MOTEL STYX

MICHELLE VON ESCHEN
AND JONATHAN BUTCHER

Praise for
Michelle von Eschen's Works

"von Eschen crafts haunting short stories of quiet horror through the lens of loss and grief."
-Bob Foster, *City of Geek*

When You Become a Body
"This darkly comedic exploration of grief was a definite page turner. Other readers have said it has a Black Mirror feel and I definitely see that. Would have fit nicely in Amazon's Forward Collection with Blake Crouch and Paul Tremblay. Well written and worth the read!"
-Duncan Ralston, author of *Woom*

Old Farmhouses of the North
"Post-apocalypse gothic vibes...lonely, desolate, cold, dusty, windswept, and atmospheric..."
-Christine Morgan, author of *Spermjackers from Hell*

"...among the very best dark fiction I read this year. Quite plainly, this woman can WRITE. Her prose is rich, metaphorical, poetic, and beautifully depressing."
-Tylor James, author of *Matters Most Macabre*

This is How We Burn
"Gorgeous writing with no clumsy exposition; it flowed so well and invested the reader in the story."
-Lucy Leitner, author of *Bad Vibrations*

Mistakes I Made During the Zombie Apocalypse
"slick and clever..."
-Peter Clines, author of *14* and *The Fold*

Praise for
Jonathan Butcher's Works

"Truly a forefront author in today's Extreme scene."
-Edward Lee
Bram Stoker Award-winning author

"A master of transgressive horror."
-Kristopher Triana
Splatterpunk Award-winning author

Your Loved Ones Will Die First
"One of the most grippingly violent books I've ever read."
-L. Andrew Cooper
Horrific Scribblings

What Good Girls Do (Elizabeth #1)
"Brilliant. Brutal. Difficult to read. Hard to put down."
-Duncan Ralston, author of *Woom*

What Good Men Do (Elizabeth #2)
"A tragic, brutal, and relentless masterpiece."
-Paula D. Ashe
Shirley Jackson Award-winning author

Something Very Wrong
"Hit after hit in this collection, not a single story failed for me."
-Megan Stockton, author of *Bluejay*

978-1-7376875-6-6
Copyright © 2024 Michelle Butcher, Jonathan Butcher,
and WtD Books

Cover design by Michelle Butcher

Book design and formatting by Michelle Butcher

Any similarity to persons living, dead, or undead is
purely coincidental.

For Jörg

Set the mood with our curated
Motel Styx Spotify Playlist

"

Every man to his taste. Mine is for corpses.

"

- Henri James Blot

Day One

Motel Styx

"

Who knows where it began? First I remember was hearing about the ColdKiss challenge, which was quickly banned on TikTok and YouTube for obvious reasons, where teens would dig up graves to get footage of themselves embracing corpses. Viral trends clearly unlocked something in the American consciousness because...well, look where we are now.

"

**- Natalie Simmons,
Sociologist and President of the Chicago School
of Contemporary Sexuality**

Goodbye

Ellis scowls into the mirror of the rumbling airplane's bathroom, preparing once again to read his dead wife's final words.

Craving reassurance that he's made the right choice—because let's face it, this is insane—he raises the letter and recites the familiar sentences in his mind.

Ellis,

You were always saying you wanted me to toughen up, to grow a pair, to stop wasting my life. I tried so hard to be who you wanted. I changed and gave up so much. I loved you, Ellis. I still love you, but last month broke me and there's no coming back from it. I'm done trying.

Don't come looking for me.

Ellis stops reading before he reaches the end, his emotions threatening to boil over into the confined space.

"You're better than that, Ellis," he tells his mirror self. "You're better than that."

He walks the aisle back to his shitty economy seat, where a large man with bad breath and a worse suit hangs over the armrest, snoring. The sight aggravates Ellis, as he'd have more space if he could afford Business Class, but his thoughts remain on his late wife.

How could she have done this to him? What could have possessed her to be so cruel, and while he's grieving for her, too? It cheapened their relationship. They deserve a better ending, so he's taking the situation into his own hands.

He tucks the letter into his carry-on and pulls out his phone to read something more hopeful: the reason why he's on the plane at all. The middle of a message exchange he'd had through his wife's Instagram with an insider waiting for him at his destination, reads:

I can help you get her back.

"Welcome to Texas," the pilot announces on the intercom shortly after the plane lands. "Where the state motto is 'Friendship'. I sure hope she treats you nicely."

Motel Styx

"

After weighing up the potential environmental health impact against the rising tide of chaos we have seen in our labs, morgues, and places of burial in recent years, it is my recommendation that the Lazarus Act is instated. Give these people somewhere to go.

"

- Dr. Stephen Wu,
On the Utility of the Dead; An Analysis of the Recreational Use of Human Bodies

---

Approach

A rock hits the hood of Ellis' rental car.

"Corpse fucker!" a shrill voice screams.

Countless bodies swarm the vehicle, blocking out the sun. Their modestly-clothed forms drag across his windows as he creeps along, giving him closeup views of pit stains and cross necklaces. If there were fewer of these cretins then Ellis might have gotten out and found the one who'd insulted him, but the mob is mad with anger and fueled by piety. He isn't about to face several dozen Christian protesters. His own, albeit godless, mission is far more important. And what would Jesus think of his flock? Swearing at a stranger, hurling insults and rocks?

Hypocrites, Ellis thinks.

A man on a motorbike rides up to the group and drags a heavy circle around them, herding the rabble into an even tighter throng around Ellis' vehicle, before tipping him a wave and driving up Yellow Bell Lane, the road that Ellis is trying to take.

"Asshole!" Ellis bellows, honking his horn.

It does little to frighten the zealots.

He wipes a hand across his sweaty forehead as more bodies of the devout press against the black sedan; sunburnt flesh on sun-baked metal. Snarling, he accelerates.

"Move or be moved," he mutters through clenched teeth.

A newly orphaned sign flops across the windshield. *Necrophilia is Sin!* it screams, as it slides out of view. Another takes its place, begging he *Let the dead rest!*

Despite Ellis' urgency to reach where he's heading, he actually agrees with them. His destination is a nest for sickos and degenerates who need to take a good hard look in the mirror. People so scared of rejection from the living, they seek company with the dead—but Ellis can't reveal his true thoughts; not to these freaks, not to anyone.

Up until he'd met the protesters, his journey from the airport was easy. No barriers, speed traps, or heavy traffic slowed his drive to the middle of nowhere. Tumbleweeds of dried Russian thistle alone had kept him company on the monotonous, dusty track of Highway 90. Only a sideways glance from the long-bearded postmaster he'd queried for directions at the nearest town— Valentine, 20 miles north— gave any hint that Ellis was heading somewhere questionable.

Merl, the owner of said questionable establishment, warned Ellis about the RV full of religious nuts who'd taken up camp just after the turnoff. His insider and secret contact, Veronika, hadn't mentioned them at all.

"Push through 'em," Merl'd said. "As willing and eager as they are to meet their lord, they won't die for Him. Too scared that their earthly remains will end up on one o' my slabs!"

Ellis lays on the gas, throwing gravel and dirt into the faces of those on the outskirts of the crowd.

Fuck 'em, he thinks as he breaks free of the horde. Let them note his license plate, live-tweet their disgust, and upload the photos they'd tried to snap of his face. The rental company at the airport promised that the car's heavily tinted windows would protect his anonymity, and the Christians' fear of the motel wouldn't find any of them following him farther.

A collection of buildings appears on the horizon, and Ellis follows a wispy wake of dust left hanging in the air by the unhelpful motorcyclist.

Merl said to follow Yellow Bell Lane until "it begins to end", but Ellis hadn't understood the comment until now, when he notices the pavement disappearing in patches, buried by the drifting desert sand and dirt. Even the gravel lane seems unsure whether it should breach the premises ahead.

Motel Styx

Depraved

Doesn't even deserve one-star! This is a den of capital-S Sin! Motel Styx is a gathering place for sickos and the city of Valentine should rise up against it! Lock the doors and throw away the keys!

Arrival

Rising from the dried out tumbleweeds, the spiky chollas and yucca, and opposite a generic-looking diner, at first Motel Styx looks like any other roadside resting place: a sun-faded soda machine, rows of identical single-windowed rooms, a huge, flickering neon sign, and a cluster of sand-coated vehicles in the parking lot.

Ellis slows and the first strange details of the venue appear.

The bumper sticker on the back of a parked sedan reads, *Dead girls don't say no!*

On the main building, bricks fill the holes where exterior entrances to the rooms once stood, and bars cover the accommodation windows, which are as heavily tinted as those on Ellis' rental car.

No residents sit outside their rooms, but a guy in navy blue coveralls rolls a new coat of dark magenta paint over graffiti on one end of the building. *Defilers!* it screams, in dripping black letters.

At the center of the complex's grounds, a man and a woman take a flirtatious selfie with a 12-foot skeleton, an ominous sentinel partially hidden by the Motel Styx sign. Beyond the couple, four guys clutching beer bottles totter and laugh around an open coffin, which is propped to standing against the base of the sign. It reminds Ellis of a lonely roadside attraction, but if you'd seen the news or read a paper in the last year you'd know this is much more than some kitsch tourist trap.

Ellis continues to survey the motel. A large warehouse-like structure rises behind the flat-top roof of the building. He eyes the behemoth, knowing exactly what it keeps in its mouth.

"Welcome to hell," he mumbles. "Enjoy your stay."

The couple and the group of men watch Ellis' car as it passes. Despite the tinted windows, he speeds up to escape their prying and turns to the right down a small road that leads around the back of the motel. Not far down the side of the building, a high security fence extends out into the distance, blocking his advancement forward. It reminds him of a prison, only this fence is meant to keep people *out*. He drives up to a gate bearing a sign which reads *Members and Staff Only Beyond This Point.*

Members. This exclusive club his dead wife has forced him to join.

Ellis flicks the A/C as high as it will go, blasting himself with cool air to dry his nervous sweat. He checks his hair in the rearview mirror and straightens the tie that's been hellbent on choking him like some corporate noose from the moment he put it on. He looks unlike his usual self: his stylish black hair falls in sweaty streaks across his brow, and his generally composed eyes look tired yet skittish. As a personal trainer in the real world his appearance generally reflects his brand, but he can't imagine it working as a great advertisement today.

"You are still a fucking king," he says to his reflection, focusing on his jawline and natural good looks rather than his disarray. "You're better than that *and* you love this. You've done it before. You're a corpse connoisseur. *Sell* it, Ellis."

No sooner than he has finished his pep talk, a mustached man in cowboy boots, black velvet pants, a red silk dress shirt, and a Stetson emerges from an undercover parking area. Ellis recognizes him by the description his contact Veronika had given him, as well as from the images accompanying the many news articles he'd read—*Ex-Mortician Turns Bigger Profit From the Dead* and *Owner of Love Motel for Necrophiles Faces Legal Troubles After Opening Day*.

The man holds up a hand in greeting and points down to the sand beneath his feet as he approaches the driver's side of the car. Ellis drops his window and flashes the membership badge he'd purchased online.

"Ah! Mr. Macintosh, the man from New York!" he says, squinting against the sunlight and the dusty desert breeze.

"You must be Merl." Ellis nods towards the dents in the hood. "Hell of a welcome party."

"Yeah, there was a reason I mentioned them. Next time, take the shuttle. It's already beat to shit, and I'm afraid we don't cover damages to private vehicles."

Next time. Ellis laughs in his head, then shrugs. "It's a rental. Insured. I've just never seen aggression like that at any of the other venues."

Merl raises an eyebrow. "Not even Canada? You said you'd been there, and I'm told they have it far worse than we do."

Not missing a beat, Ellis says, "Not when I visited. Very polite and friendly—until someone mentions the hockey."

Merl grins and gives a courteous half laugh. "Well anyway, you're here safely! Your flight okay?"

"Hard to complain about First Class."

"Wonderful! Okay, that barcode on your badge gets you access to anywhere that you see one of these." Merl points to a small black box on a pole and produces a badge of his own to scan. The gates slide open. "Pull through and pick a spot."

Ellis parks between what he assumes is the shuttle—a pockmarked black van missing half its rear bumper, no doubt with pieces of Christian flesh embedded in its grille—and the motorcycle he saw on the road, its engine still ticking in cooldown from its journey.

He glances around. Beyond the chain link fence that surrounds the parking area, several large, droning fans protrude from the wall of the building behind the motel. He stares at the cooling unit and feels new beads of sweat build on his brow. His wife could be on the other side of that wall, her death on pause for the whims of sickos who can't find someone breathing to fuck.

Merl mistakes Ellis' silence and fixed gaze for admiration.

"It's one of the largest walk-ins in the state," the proprietor says with pride. "Thing of beauty. Holds up to

300 bodies, easy. Need any help with your bag?"

Ellis tries not to imagine so many corpses, but fails. His throat tightens. He looks down at the hastily packed case on the back seat and waves a 'no thanks'.

Maybe he's in over his head. Does he really think he can convince *this* guy, with his Texas swagger and intense passion for his bizarre work? Can Ellis *really* pass as one of these so-called 'necs'? He takes a deep breath and resolves once more that he has no choice. On the other end of this charade lies the still form of a woman who promised to be with him and him alone.

He drags his rolling hardshell over the tiny crushed rocks of the parking area, acid burning in his stomach.

"Now, remember, you signed a waiver," Merl says. "You agree to hold Motel Styx and all its great and good employees—myself included—free from prosecution. We do everything we can to keep this place safe and sound. We can't be held liable if you catch something from the bodies. We recommend you protect yourself at all times and we provide unlimited free condoms, but we're not going to stretch the damn things over your junk ourselves, now are we? So you enter under your own free will, and... yadda yadda yadda."

Ellis' armpits dampen. It's real. All of it. "Do we have to do this outside?"

"The heat out here puts the pressure on!"

"I already signed the contract. I've agreed to everything."

"Apologies, but surely you've read the stories the press have been making up about this place. Can't blame me for being cautious!" Merl gestures towards another black box, this one attached to a coffin-shaped door labeled *Members Only*. "Give it a go."

Ellis scans his badge. The lock beeps open.

Out of the frying pan and into the freaky fucking fire, he thinks.

"

Brothers and sisters: we have a new enemy in our midst. The devil, that old serpent, is no longer content to claim the flesh and souls of the damned, but their rotting remains as well! Please, join me in prayer, lest we ourselves are also consumed by this latest abomination!

"

**- Pastor Jeremiah Tuck
(later excommunicated after accusations
of corpse desecration)**

Motel Styx

Grateful to be out of the scorching Texas heat, Ellis follows Merl down a dimly lit hall, its walls covered in red velvet and adorned with black-framed photographs of naked figures in poses both upright and prone. It's hard to tell if they're alive or dead, but judging by their dulled eyes and the establishment in which they're displayed, Ellis assumes the latter.

Merl looks back at him. "I must admit, I was mighty impressed when you mentioned that you'd been to the Corpse Capsule Motel in Tokyo. Savin' up to head there myself. Those Japanese businessmen love their booze, but they love their bodies even more."

There's no way in hell Ellis would climb into a glorified coffin with a decaying corpse, but at his contact Veronika's urging he'd done his research and memorized the details of the four other love motels around the world catering to necrophiles—colloquially called *necrotels*.

"My consulting firm takes me all over the place," Ellis says. "I've lucked out a few times and been placed near one of your sister establishments, if that's the right term. As I mentioned in my application, I've been to the ones in Cairo and Toronto as well. Just got Holland to go after here and I'll have completed the set."

Merl laughs. "An honor to be associated with them, but the other necrotels have been in the business for almost half a decade. 18 months is enough to get things rolling over here, but Congress dragged their heels for so long passing the Lazarus Act, it'll be an uphill climb until I'm as successful as the others. Still, I'm on the right side of history, as I'm sure you'll agree."

"Of course," Ellis replies, hating having to pander to this man. "Nice to see such passion for your business."

Merl stops and turns to face him. "It's in my blood! My father was a mortician, so my brother and I grew up around death. Hell, I lost my virginity to a girl in my school after she died in a drowning accident. Someone who wouldn't even give me the time of day when she was alive, but nude before me on a fucking platter..."

Ellis hides his disgust at the delight Merl has for his transgressions with the dead. He didn't expect the man to open up like this, especially after just meeting, but being into this sort of thing must be lonely. He dips his head and allows Merl to continue.

"Until now, us necs didn't have anywhere welcoming to go, and some folks resorted to terrible things. While I don't approve, thank God for the fella who broke into the body farm and destroyed all that research. That sped Congress up, for sure."

Ellis had read about that sick fuck at the body farm, too, but rather than tell Merl what he really thinks, he wipes his brow and pulls his shirt from his chest. "Sure feels better in here than out there."

"You can finally breathe again. In more ways than one! The Members Lounge is through there." Merl points to a door on their right, then leads him into an open vestibule ahead with many hallways and doors branching off from it. Merl gestures for Ellis to look around. "The entire interior, barring the lobby and front offices, gift shop, and the staff lounge, is kept extra-cool to help the bodies last longer. Any room that might have a corpse in it, we take every step we can to slow the rot. And it isn't just the temperature—we have all sorts of other means and measures to ensure that our customers get their money's worth."

Ellis freezes as a man in a robe pushes an occupied wheelchair down one of the long halls toward them.

The rider is a woman, seemingly nude but for a matching robe, with one of her paled nipples poking from its edge. Her toes drag on the carpet and her head lies over the backrest, causing her mouth to hang open toward the ceiling in a quiet perpetual yawn. It's her eyes that trouble Ellis most: crystal-clear but unfocused, like polished marbles. She shows no signs of concern or life, a love doll for all intents and purposes, but still the man repositions her feet on the footrests for the duration of the ride, perhaps to avoid carpet burn and protect his investment.

Ellis has seen dead bodies—his mother's in the morgue, his wife's on the bathroom floor—but they'd been clothed, covered, still, not flaunted and flitted about. He swallows his shock, a thick ball in his throat, and feigns interest in a photograph of a man and woman entwined around a skeleton.

Merl nods to the man pushing the wheelchair, who keeps his head lowered and his gaze straight ahead as he passes.

"Chairs are available by request if you feel like taking your companions to the lounge or to the theater room, Ellis."

"That's...great. I hadn't even considered it." *Because why would I have ever thought of carting a corpse around for company?*

"You better start dreaming a bit, man. You're finally here!"

Ellis can't help but ask. "Merl...her eyes...how were they..."

"So clear? That's one of our signature traits, here at Motel Styx! Each of our companions, unless otherwise requested, is fitted with glass replacements to match the precise tone and shade they had in life. Otherwise they have a tendency to go milky and lose that sheen, pretty fast."

Ellis can't help but picture his wife goggling at him with two brand-new, glimmering eyes.

Merl looks at his watch. "You're a *little* earlier than I'd expected, so housekeeping is just finishing up your room. Would you like some refreshment in the bar while you wait? On the house?"

"I wasn't expecting to wait. How about the tour you

promised on the phone?"

His contact Veronika drew Ellis a map of the labyrinthine motel, but seeing a picture of something and actually walking its distances are completely different things. He needs to know exactly where his wife is, and how to reach her.

Merl blinks. "Keen, aren't you, Mr. Macintosh? You just got here after...what?...a day's journey, and you want to crack right on with things."

Veronika also told Ellis how to counter Merl's suspicious nature. *You'll have to butter him up*, he remembers her saying. "You're the newest necrotel and I've read about your fine tastes. I've heard that Motel Styx has the most up-to-date systems and services, so I want to see them all."

It's solid intel. The right approach opens up Merl's face with glee. "Well, I like a man who goes after what he wants. Reminds me of myself. I've got a call to make though so give me a few minutes. Take a gander at the gift shop while you wait. I'll store your bag behind reception so you don't have to lug it around."

Ellis watches Merl roll his hardshell case into a side room by the front desk and then pick up the landline phone there. The proprietor seems affable, but Ellis isn't charmed. All that this blustering pervert represents is an obstacle standing between Ellis and his wife.

She's mine, you bastard, he thinks.

Motel Styx

Great gift shop

Long drive for a gag gift, but totally worth it: it literally made him 'gag'!

The Gift Shop

Playing the part of an interested browser, Ellis grudgingly pushes open the door to the gift shop. The room has all the fixings he'd expect: a spinner rack packed with postcards and books, shelves of souvenir trinkets, and baskets of candies and plush toys unreasonably marked up—but, like the outside of the motel, the devil is in the details.

Bone-shaped candies and gummies formed into brains and rotting cocks sit snug inside small, plastic baggies. Keychains and air fresheners dangling from metal prongs take new, unexpected shapes, die-cut into toe tags and coffins. A spinner rack offers customized gravestone magnets. *Rest in Pleasure* they read, followed by an alphabetical collection of common names from the last few decades. Ellis scans the 'E's, and for once is glad that his is a name not often emblazoned on such gifts.

He examines the postcards, then the posters which feature images of the giant skeleton out front, artist's renditions of the stages of human decomposition, handy guides to some of the sexual positions one can take with a corpse, autopsy diagrams, and other morbid illustrations. Nearby, slogans adorn bumper stickers and t-shirts, saying things like *Once You Go Slack, You Never Go Back!*, and *I Fucked a Corpse at Motel Styx and All I Got Was This Stupid T-Shirt*. One for the more intellectually inclined reads: *Motel Styx: Where la petite mort meets la grande mort!*

The motel logo—its name inside a coffin-shaped border with the tagline *Best beds, best bodies!*—is on everything, from shot glasses, to condom packaging, to the protruding ends of butt plugs, to the metal stamp in the penny pressing machine in the corner. Ellis collected those pennies when he was a kid, his mom dragging him to every corner of the United States. *God, if she knew I was here*, he thinks. She'd slap him across the head before handing him 50 cents for one of *these* defaced coins.

"Need a hand at all?"

Ellis startles and nearly knocks a bone-shaped dildo from its shelf. He'd thought he was alone in the retail space, but in one corner a pale girl stands behind the register. A poster for the movie *Nekromantik* covers the wall behind her, making it appear as though the drooping eyeball of the putrid corpse might detach and plop onto her head. The young woman had been so still and silent, Ellis assumed she was some kind of life-size doll.

"Are you finding what you're looking for?" she asks politely.

"No, I'm really not," Ellis replies. "You wouldn't carry it, not in here anyway."

The girl shrugs and picks up a cellphone from the counter.

Now aware he isn't alone, he self-consciously sniffs

a formaldehyde-scented candle that smells like broken branches, and shakes a toe bone inside its small glass vial. While some might find such a place grimly amusing or at least curious, Ellis takes deep breaths to avoid becoming furious. It's all so proud of its degeneracy. So tacky. So... *normalized*.

His heart thuds in his chest, but inside it's breaking. He glances around, shaking his head and thinking of his wife. *You really know how to hurt me, Emeley.*

"You okay there, Mr. Macintosh?" Merl asks, appearing in the doorway and nodding 'hello' to the shop attendant. "Find anything good?"

Ellis wipes a shirt sleeve across his eyes and brow. "It's a nice touch." He fondles a keychain in the shape of an urn. "Do members really buy this stuff?"

"Nope! Not a lick of it! But we get a lot of folks who hear about us on a blog or on the news. Lots of interest on social media. They drive all the way out here and get disappointed when I can't let them onto the rest of the property or show them a body, so that's when I show them all this merch they can take back to impress their friends at home. They eat this shit right up. Ain't that right, Molly?"

The young woman at the register looks up from her phone and smiles. "It's all over TikTok." She turns her phone around to show Ellis the screen. On it, a man laughs as he holds the bone dildo against his crotch and pretends to masturbate it.

Ellis wipes his hands on his pants.

Merl continues. "Once I get a bit more organized we'll start taking orders online at motelstyx.com and ship directly from the motel here. The novelty of it hasn't escaped me. It's a real cash cow."

"Two different revenue streams, nice," Ellis says, growing tired of Merl's spiel and his own requisite interest. "Ready to show me around?"

"Sure thing. Mind you, not many guests want the full tour so I might be a bit rusty."

"

Over the last three years we've seen an exponential increase in the use of necro-related hashtags, such as #LightsOnNobodyHome, #ColdLovin, #CoffinRocker and #MorgueRat. Whether it's a case of necs always having been here, or the explosion of an underground phenomenon due to global exposure, the trend is gaining popularity.

"

- 'The Rise of the Loving Dead,' USA Tonight

The Guided Tour

Merl leads Ellis back through a secure door into the vestibule behind the office. He points at a closed entrance on the far wall.

"Staff only, just like it says. Any black box beyond it can't be opened with your member badge." He holds the door open for Ellis. "Welcome to 'behind the curtain' as they say—this is the real guts of the place. We'll start at the back, where it all begins."

Through the portal, the cold hits Ellis and he pulls his jacket closed over his shirt. Here, plain white walls and cold steel give the illusion of a sterilized medical ward. Ellis imagines this area as the cogs of a machine, all business and nothing like the heavily decorated and stylized motel proper. The scent of bleach and something quite like the formaldehyde candle floats in pockets in the hallway, the lingering ghosts of the recently cleaned dead. They pass several doors on their way down the hall to a non-descript door leading into a large, open room. Ellis counts each door carefully, in an effort to cement the layout in his mind.

Merl swipes his badge and the door unlocks. He points to a large metal entrance of a loading dock. "The donated bodies—and I say 'donated' loosely, as each one is purchased and the payout released to the estate upon death—come in already serial-numbered on refrigerated trucks, and we unload them here, check they've got all their documents in order. We also take a look at the general state of the body itself. Then, this cold conveyor system brings them to the fridge where those fans you were admiring work their asses off to protect my investments. The bodies stay nice and chilled for the entire trip—gotta keep them in their prime for as long as possible, 'cause we're battling the clock when it comes to decomp. Did you know, some people think the ancient Greeks and Egyptians used to let bodies rot in the sun, so nec embalmers couldn't have their fun? Such a waste."

Ellis can believe it and if he'd had his way, his wife would have been left untouchable, either putrefying in the earth or burned to ashes. He views the meandering belt, still for the moment, and wonders if Emeley, stripped of her name, wedding ring, and clothing, reduced to a serial number and contractual consent, had already journeyed down its length.

"The conveyor belt actually gave me the idea for the

name of the motel. It's like a river, carrying the dead to their next destination."

"Making you the ferryman?" Ellis asks, wryly.

"The ferryman, the boat, the coin. Yeah. I'm a bit of the rest of it, I guess."

The joy of Merl's expression bites Ellis harder than the cold. Ellis will ensure, soon enough, that the smugness is wiped from the man's face.

"The clipboard there lists the requests of all our motel guests. When the bodies come, I can pre-mark them for members with specific preferences. Give them a call and a chance to have them before anyone else, if they aren't booked in with us already that is. Lots of members consider the motel a home away from home. We've got a few long stays, too."

Trying to sound casual, Ellis asks, "Speaking of preferences, do you have contracts from people who...take their own lives?"

"Oh yeah all sorts, but I've got strict rules about the state of the bodies. Can't have any visible wounds, gotta come with a clean bill of health—communicable diseases and such—up until the time of death. And if they're for use by the general Styx populace, they've gotta be embalmed."

Hope blooms in Ellis' mind. *She could be turned away.*

Merl continues. "If a body arrives and it don't fit the bill to be a decent companion, like it comes in all chewed-up, pumped full of holes, sliced up or some other shit, then I might have it returned to next of kin and demand reimbursement."

Ellis wonders who Emeley named as her next of kin. "No imperfect fruit then," he says, almost to himself.

"No bruises."

"Well, it's not so cut-and-dry as all that," Merl says. "Our talented staff can smooth out certain blemishes, so..."

Ellis' patience snaps. "Well, do you accept damaged bodies or not?"

Merl looks cautious. "I thought you'd read the contract?"

"Sorry. I'm just curious, that's all."

A light of realization pops on in Merl's eyes. "Ah, in your application you mentioned that you don't mind 'em rough! When you did, it sounded like maybe you were used to second-rate stiffs. I just thought, no sir, not here at Motel Styx! *Best beds, best bodies* is our motto! Especially for a VIP!"

As the Texan cheerfully smacks Ellis' arm, Ellis holds on to the brief moment of hope he'd felt. According to Veronika's last messages, his wife is still in transit, barreling down a freeway in the back of a semi, frost forming on her unmoving eyelashes.

Maybe she looks bad enough to be turned away. Maybe she won't even end up here.

It would make Ellis' trip so much easier if the ferryman refuses to take her, if Merl turns the goddamn boat around and dumps her back on the shore she came from.

Ellis has no way of knowing for certain though, no tracking number, no permission to know.

"I really do like them with a little damage," he says to cover his bases, pointing to the clipboard and playing up his 'nec with a fetish' persona. "No point in refusing them. Add that to my preferences."

Merl shrugs. "Maybe you'll like our wetrooms, then? You can do what you want with the bodies in there."

"I don't want..." Ellis trails off. "So do the ones that you don't consider up to snuff always go back to the family?"

"It's all stipulated by the contract. And if it isn't mentioned, then it depends on the next-of-kin's wishes. We hold the body and wait for them to decide. We can send 'em to a funeral home, or, for a small fee, we'll cremate them right here." Merl nods toward a door beyond the winding conveyor belt, its plain surface labeled *Crematory*. "I've baked a lot of 'imperfect fruit' in that oven. Same with the overripe and used-up ones. There's only one place the bodies that become companions here at Motel Styx end up, and it's right behind that door."

More words perch on Ellis' dry lips, but he can't just inquire if Emeley would go straight to the crematory—contracts with the donors prohibit family members from requesting details about their passed loved ones once they arrive at the motel, unless the body donors expressly allow for it. Emeley opted for privacy. He knew that much. She'd shut him out. He locks his despair behind a straight face.

Merl cocks his head, trying to read Ellis' expression.

Ellis forces a smile.

"Don't worry about it!" Merl cries. "We've got an amazing few days lined up and you'll be hard-pressed to be disappointed when you see the three women I'll be pulling for you. I'm your wingman, man! In fact, one of those beauts is in there right now." He points to a heavy-duty sliding door. "That's the fridge, though I think of it as the pantry, but I know that ain't the right word. No one eats 'em—that'd be *crazy*! I can keep them for years if I want, but if one gets popular and stays out of the fridge more often than not, it'll start to go downhill much sooner."

"Can I see inside?"

A broad, shit-eating grin stretches across Merl's face. "Didn't think I'd leave you in suspense, did ya?"

The Texan adjusts his hat and touches his keycard to the black electronic lock. It bleeps and he tugs open the sliding door with a clunk and a swish. A cloud of icy condensate rolls out.

Merl tuts. "The temp climbs and drops. She's colder than she should be today, but that's better than the other way around."

Dozens, if not hundreds, of black zip-up bags lie stacked four-high on wheeled shelving units. The sliding metal layers make Ellis think of baking trays stacked inside an oven.

He remembers his wife's small lips and thinks of them pressed against the thick plastic, her eyes, perhaps not yet replaced with glass replicas, staring into the darkness of her cold storage tomb.

What kind of animals keep you on tap like this, Emeley? Tucked away like fucking leftovers? And you asked *for this?*

The urge to dash into the room and start unzipping bags almost overwhelms him, but the amount he's paid and risked to get here isn't worth giving into such a haphazard impulse. He has to stay measured, controlled in his approach. He stores the intrusive thought and shivers.

"Chilly, ain't it?" Merl says. "Or was that excitement? So many tantalizing possibilities in here." He chuckles and drags the door closed. "Moving along..."

As Merl turns away and heads for the next door, Ellis watches the Texan's wide, arrogant gait, and wants to throw a solid punch into his fat-rolled neck.

"Behind here we have the prep room," Merl says, as he scans his badge once more and pushes the swinging door inward. "The cadavers are brought from the fridge to cooling boar– Goddamnit, Arnie! I said 'not on the clock'!"

The body of an older woman, maybe in her sixties, lies nude on a steel table, cloudy eyes pointing at the ceiling. Her knees are raised and spread, the thatched forest of her pubis on full display. At her head, a tall, gangly man stands hunched with his apron hanging behind him like a cape. His pants are unzipped and he holds his cock in his hand, rubbing it vigorously. A bottle of lotion drips from its pump onto the corpse's hair.

Ellis steps back, repulsed.

"How many times, Arnie?" Merl yells, but he sounds like a teacher admonishing a mischievous pupil instead of a boss witnessing a sackable offense.

Arnie pulls his apron back around so it tents at the crotch, and hangs his head. "Sorry, Merl."

"Put your dick away and clean her up. Room 15 is waiting, and you've got the body stack to prepare for the man who likes to be smothered!"

Red-faced, Arnie zips back up and busies himself with the body, rearranging her into a more respectful, straight-legged pose. He smooths the leaked lotion into her hair almost lovingly.

Merl looks at Ellis with a 'boys will be boys' expression, and talks about Arnie's past as though the horny attendant isn't there.

"I poached Arnie from the funeral home in town. They caught him with a body while he was prepping it for a funeral, so when they fired him, I snapped him up.

You wouldn't be able to tell from what you just saw—or that story—but he's a hell of a hire. Knows exactly how to treat the bodies and clean 'em up—when he isn't dirtying them himself, that is."

Appalled, Ellis forces a chuckle and a few words of feigned agreement. "Before the Lazarus Act, if we weren't denying our impulses, we were breaking the law to chase them. It's good we don't have to hide anymore. Though I *will* ask that anyone sent to my room doesn't get Arnie's...special attentions."

"Of course! Of course! You have my word. He doesn't mess with the VIP bodies. Isn't that right, Arnie?"

"Yes, Mr. Bonvante."

"Anyway, as I was saying. They are kept on cooling boards while they are cleaned, pre- or post-rental. The cooling boards buy us even more time with the body. Now come on—there's plenty left to see..."

Merl takes Ellis through the rest of the processing rooms, storage areas, and a small staff area with lockers and a drip coffee machine. There are fewer employees present than he'd expected, and Ellis takes it all in as a distracted bystander, thinking of what he'd do to Arnie if he found out he'd touched his wife.

Back in the main body of the motel the tour continues, and Ellis is surprised when his guts finally settle. He listens to Merl talk, imagining he's learning about the inner workings of any other business: the absurd themed rooms, the choice of bodies, the different price tiers available.

"We've even got a room for Class 1 couples wanting to play up to the nec fantasy, without any actual contact with the dead," Merl continues. "As long as they sign a waiver and show they're healthy, we have a patent-pending blend of drugs and extreme cold that can *almost* replicate death. The firm I funded calls it SynthaMort! Means hubbies and wives can do as they please with their partners, as though they've already kicked the bucket! Dead action role playing!" Merl's eyes are wide with pride. "Get it?"

"Instead of live action, yeah. DARP-ing just doesn't have the same ring to it."

"I'll agree with you there!" Merl pats Ellis on the back, then leads him down the other side of the motel, along a new corridor he hasn't visited yet.

As they walk, Ellis summons the will to compliment Merl again: "I have to say, you've really thought of everything. I'm impressed."

"It's not all rainbows and butterflies: we're never less than knee-deep in lawsuits or investigations. This month we've got the frat boy suicide after a hazing involving a corpse here at the motel. Guess he couldn't live with himself after porking a dead girl. Fucking pussy. Family is suing for emotional damages."

"Shit."

"At least he didn't kill himself on the property. That woulda been a whole other mess. As it is, we'll win that case. All parties involved were consenting. It's the fraternity they should be going after. *They* booked the cabin." He sniffs with distaste. "And you won't be seeing those on the tour, as they're all occupied at the moment."

Ellis shrugs.

"Then we had the serial killer dumping bodies on a corner of our land, thinking he could hide his crimes."

Ellis manages a half-hearted joke. "Seems like it could have been a nice setup? He does the dirty work, and you get a free body to sell."

Merl chuckles, but his long mustache twitches with concern. "No, ya see, contracts are important because consent is important. *Respect* is important."

Unconvinced, Ellis thinks of Arnie and the dead woman. How much respect was that?

Merl concludes, "We consider this closer to post-mortem sex work than some underground dark-web murder-room."

Ellis bristles.

He's calling Emeley a whore.

The urge to punch the proprietor returns, but Ellis quells it by encouraging Merl to continue with the story. "So what happened to the serial killer?"

"Cops traced our local Bundy-wannabe pretty quick, but they scared a lot of members away while they were swooping around the grounds like vultures." He readjusts his hat and turns a corner into a passage with walls lined with autopsy photos. "It's been an interesting 18 months."

Someone clears their throat behind them and Ellis and Merl part to let Arnie through with an occupied gurney. Arnie stops outside a door with the number '15' on it and knocks. Ellis can't see who opens the door, but he hears them. He wonders if this delivered body is the same one they just caught Arnie molesting.

"You're late!" a man yells from inside. "You're wasting my Viagra!"

Arnie backs out of the room, mumbling apologies.

"Send that man a bottle of wine, Arnie!" Merl snaps.

"Don't bother!" the angry guest bellows. "Just leave us in peace!"

The door slams closed.

Satan worshippers

I'd give no stars if I could! These people are defiling human beings! Who knows what else they're up to in those rooms! Sign the petition to close this abomination!

Interlude:

Room 15 —The Outcast

Wine does nothing for Clarence; nothing like a dead woman in a morgue does for him, anyway.

There was a time when he'd felt guilty for his urges towards the departed, but the dead are beyond caring about anything he does to them. It's the living who take issue with it, so in return the man takes issue with the living. All that noise, all that fussing, and all those meaningless arguments about what's acceptable and what isn't. All their squabbles fade into silence when the old man is alone with a good, cold, *quiet* cadaver.

Clarence rolls the gurney toward the metal trayed table in the center of the room, his joints creaking and the wheels squeaking. As he reaches the edge of the table, he pulls the sheet beneath the older body, sliding her from one horizontal plane to another but leaving her covered for now. It's a movement that's second nature, one he performed thousands of times in his old role as a mortician. He'd once assumed that he'd have found fellow necs and allies in the trade, but he never met another corpse-fondler in all his years of service, and that suited him just fine. He's sure that trades such as his, alongside the emergency services and pathologists, attract necs just like the cloth and the cub scouts attract pedophiles, but he's learnt that there are more professionals out there than perverts.

Clarence retired before the Lazarus Act was instated, effectively drying up his dating pool for years, but then the law changed and Merl opened membership for Motel Styx. That was one of the best uses he ever found for his Social Security check: room, board, and bodies.

He circles the woman on the table and, sighing with pleasure, pulls the sheet off her. Mid-sixties, he'd guess. Rigor mortis had been and gone, and the embalming— not to Clarence's precise tastes, but better than turning rancid—had turned her body into a tranquil, inviting playground. Something invisible killed her: her heart, her lungs, her bowels, maybe. Natural causes will sate his unnatural tastes.

"Come to spend a bit of time with me before we put you in the ground?" he says.

That same thrill he'd felt so many times before builds inside him. The fear of being caught and exposed in his perceived vileness rumbles through his body. A man meant to revere and respect the vulnerable dead, trusted to clean and beautify them, expected to honor their memory, found out to be a rapist and defiler.

Grinning, he drops his robe and the cold of the

morgue room grips him like a vise, pulling his balls closer and erecting his sagging nipples to match his Viagra-engorged penis.

"Your family won't be here for a few hours," he assures her. "Plenty of time to mess around."

He pictures the funeral parlor in an imagined nearby room, the flowers set out, an easel holding an oversized photo of the woman smiling, her eyes alive and joyful. He looks down at her dull, cloudy eyes—no glass replacements for Clarence's girls—and takes in her beauty in death.

"I'll pump you full of life," he pants. "I'll make you smile again."

He drags a small stool to the end of the table and within two steps he is able to kneel between the corpses' legs.

The resistance of the dead is all part of Clarence's foreplay: despite her being slacker than a rigor-ridden corpse, she plays coy like the others, her dead muscles tight and lacking their full range of motion. With a grunt, Clarence lifts her arms over her head, savoring the creaks and snaps as she submits to him.

"You want it, don't you? Spread it for me!"

He clears his throat and spits onto her pubic mound, then watches his saliva run down the folds of her vulva, swollen by the death process. Pressing his drug-hardened cock against the darkness between her labia, he thrusts, plunging as deep as his aged spine and hips can manage. The rocking causes her head to turn to one side, exposing the cool flesh of her neck. He lowers closer to her and kisses the arctic plain.

"No one will ever know," he whispers in her ear, as he fucks her. "I'll cum inside you and plug you up and put you in a coffin in that pretty dress they picked, and they won't know that your pussy reeks of me, is filled with me! Ahhhhhh..."

As he releases into the dead woman, he smiles, thankful for Merl's fearlessness, for standing up and exposing himself to the world's vitriol, so that less brave men like Clarence can satisfy their carnal pleasures without fear of trading their profession or reputation for a prison sentence.

"

How dare you critics suggest it's somehow immoral? These aren't grave-robbed corpses stolen in the night—they're given freely by their owners while they're still alive and capable. And how dare you deprive their grieving relatives of the money such donations reap? #LazarusAct

"

@BodyBagBlower1992, X (formerly Twitter)

———————————

The Wetrooms

"Final stop of the tour is next," Merl says to Ellis. "Saved you something wild for last."

They walk to the end of a hall, one of the long arms of the U-shaped building, to stand in front of three doors. Rooms 17-19. The lights are dimmer here at the other end of the motel than anywhere Ellis has so far visited, and tinted an eerie amber.

Merl lowers his voice when he next speaks: "These three doors hold something very special. You'll know from your travels that no other necrotel offers anything like it. We call these the wetrooms."

Ellis had read the website and the membership brochure. He knows exactly what lies behind these doors: moppable floors that slope toward drains in the center, tiled walls for easy clean-up, cutting devices, meat hooks, operating tables...rooms retrofitted for a type of torture where the victims don't scream.

Before Ellis has a chance to say he'd rather not see inside, that the mental image and the online description are enough, the door in the middle labeled '18' opens.

Merl halts.

Ellis hears him gasp.

A muscular Asian man steps into the corridor, grinning, his thick arms tattooed with snakes that coil from shoulder to wrist. Blood speckles his face and he is nude but for a plastic apron. Bits of flesh dry on the material. He grips a cordless tool with a holesaw drill bit attachment, and draws circles with it in the air that shrink smaller until they slow to a stop.

Merl raises his hands and stammers, "S...sorry to interrupt, Yamamoto. Full tour."

"You want a demonstration?" the blood-covered man asks, his manic smile widening. He opens the door further behind him, ushering them in. "I'll show you. I'll show you."

Ellis takes a step backward. "That's not necessary."

Merl places a hand on his shoulder, like a gentle warning. Despite all the Texan's bluster, Ellis has an inkling that Merl is wary of this particular guest.

"Yamamoto is one of our exhibitionist members. He likes to be watched," Merl explains, his eyes flicking between Ellis and the bloody man. "I'm sure you can appreciate a nec being able to...attain pleasure?"

Ellis nods slowly, trapped by his need to fit in and Merl's request for camaraderie. There's something more as well: a hint of fear on Merl's face. Ellis swallows, his throat as dry as the desert surrounding the motel. In a way, this is one of the reasons he's come to Motel Styx: to see what happens to the bodies.

To know that he's right to intervene.

To justify whatever he has to do to protect his wife, even now.

"Okay," he says. Hearing the weakness in his voice, he hardens his tone. "Show me."

Yamamoto's grin seems to split his face.

Motel Styx

I saw red

The wetrooms are exquisite. Equipped with everything I could want. Except maybe a chainsaw.

Yamamoto

Yamamoto holds the door, allowing Ellis to pass through a heavy cloud reeking of expensive aftershave, blood, and sex fluids. Yamamoto revs the drill as he shuts the door behind them, and Ellis manages not to jump. He stops beside Merl, who stands stiffly in the corner.

The room inside is bright, with the ceiling light and several wall-mounted strip lamps glaring across its occupants. At the center of the tiled floor on a metal embalming table, two unclothed bodies lie facing each other: a dark-skinned woman in her 20s and a light-skinned woman in her 40s. The younger body's arms are wrapped around the older body's shoulders, while the older has its stiff hands resting on the curve of the younger's backside. Unlike the glass orbs Ellis has already seen, their eyes are cloudy with death, natural and unchanged. Their jaws are slack. Their flesh is dotted with gouged glistening holes that match the size of Yamamoto's drill attachment.

Blood has sluiced down a sloped runnel at their feet

and trickled into a drain. Layered plugs of flesh, fat, and muscle lie discarded on the floor, like small towers of jellied cranberry sauce shaken free of their cans.

Ellis moves his mind to a calm space he reserves for stressful moments. He breathes evenly, accepts his raised heartbeat, and focuses on the few palatable aspects of the situation: the whir of the air-con and its coolness on his skin, and the fact that Merl seems even more unnerved than he is. But he can't help but consider who these women were before they became whatever Yamamoto's vision has morphed them into. A librarian? A soccer mom? A musician? A store clerk? When they signed the contracts willing their bodies away—ticking some box allowing use in the wetrooms—did they foresee such desecration? Power tools and ego trips, domination and dismemberment? A chill climbs his spine. Who would knowingly sign up for this?

Maybe Emeley...

Yamamoto approaches the bodies and smiles. Now with his audience, his cock stands to attention behind the transparent apron and his biceps flex as he raises the drill. He points to some of the wounds his tool has already carved: wells inside the older corpse's neck, cheek, and motherly breasts; gaps in the younger body's taut stomach, side, and upper groin. Then Yamamoto looks directly at Ellis and says, "Fuck buffet."

The man's gleeful gaze lingers on Ellis. He realizes he is expected to answer. "What?" he manages.

Irritation flickers across Yamamoto's face. He uses his free hand to mime eating. "Buffet. Fuck buffet."

Ellis turns to Merl, mystified.

Yamamoto tries again: "All you can fuck."

"He means 'buffet,'" Merl clarifies.

Yamamoto clicks his fingers. "Fuck *buffet*." He runs his hand tenderly over the lighter skinned woman's flesh, then over the other's darker tones, pausing briefly to delve into a drill-hole beside its navel. His middle finger emerges red.

Ellis almost retches. *This is what happens here*, he thinks. *This is what they'll do to Emeley and to the flesh she promised would always be mine.*

Yamamoto takes the younger body's chin and jerks it up so the vacant face looks straight at him, then places the hole-saw against the forehead. "Mind-fuck," he says, and in the glare of the room's vivid lights his eyes roll, feigning orgasmic ecstasy.

He can do anything to them, Ellis realizes. Total power. Total submission.

No one answers back.

Beneath his apron Yamamoto's hard penis twitches, dancing to the beat of his pulse. His eyes return to the younger cadaver as he holds the drill steady against her skull.

Ellis is desperate to turn away, but can't.

The drill bursts into motion, crunching and whinnying through the bone to the soft spongy brain, carving a path to allow this man to...no...*surely not...*

Ellis darts to the door, yanks it open, and leaps back into the corridor.

"Hey, where ya going?" Merl calls, following Ellis out. "Sorry—enjoy!" he tells Yamamoto, and shuts the door behind them. Looking concerned, he watches Ellis catch his breath. "Post-mortem pacifist, huh?"

"What?" Ellis asks, reeling as though he's witnessed a fatal car crash.

"Not into the violence," Merl says. "I get it. Me neither, really. Takes a special kind of nec to get pleasure from that—Class 6 necs if you want to be clinical: necromutilomaniacs—but they're more common than you'd think. Then again, you did say you don't mind your bodies being a bit beaten up... Anyway, maybe I shouldn't have taken you in there without warning you. The thing is, Mr. Yamamoto is..."

Behind the door, the drill buzzes again; a high-pitched *screeeee*.

Merl winces, removes his Stetson, scratches his scalp, and replaces the hat. "Never mind. Anyway, I apologize."

"It's fine," Ellis says. "I got light-headed, is all. I thought the bodies were all embalmed?"

"Not those for the wetrooms. Folks like Yamamoto get their kicks from cutting the bodies up and seeing the insides as they should be. As they are."

Ellis feels woozy. "Tell me my room is ready, Merl."

Terrific turndown service

This place has all the fittings you'd expect from a motel, but what really stands out is the cleanliness. Room was spotless on check-in and after a fun day spent in bed.

Interlude:

The Greenlee Suite — The Cleaner

As nasty as the place can sometimes get, being Head of Cleaning at Motel Styx is still preferable to Mona's previous role.

Spending her life clearing up the aftermath of shotgun blasts, or the Person Soup of bodies left too long without attention, had gotten to Mona in the end. The sadness of it all. A lot of others working in trauma cleanup made cruel jokes about the departed, scooping up the fleshy scraps and soaking up the gore like uneaten leftovers at a fast food restaurant, but Mona couldn't do that. Those remains were once people, and that was the only way Mona could treat them. So when an unprompted email arrived in her inbox from Merl, offering her a new position and a nice pay raise, she weighed up the pros and cons and made the jump.

The irony was, most of her wise-cracking ex-colleagues looked down on her decision to accept a contract with Motel Styx.

Mona is a certified technician, not just a cleaner, and the skills she'd learnt dealing with homicides and rotten cadavers transferred smoothly to her new job at the motel. She still deals with corpses, bodily fluids, and mutilation, but with one key difference: everyone whose earthly remains end up played-with and plundered inside these walls consented to it. That's why Mona finds no sorrow here: only bodies freely given for a fair price, and living clients finding pleasure where they had found only frustration before. Suicide and murder are products of misery and evil; Motel Styx's cadavers are bizarre instruments of joy. At least, that's how Mona rationalizes her role.

While working at Motel Styx is surface-similar to a regular maid's work at a normal motel, Mona has to be infinitely more meticulous. Take the Greenlee Suite today, for example, which she has prepared for another VIP guest.

First difference: Mona works in full personal protective equipment, or PPE, to prevent health risks. Gloves, mask, goggles, and a white bodysuit.

Second difference: Mona doesn't just strip beds, vacuum, and clear up dirty plates; she's responsible for removing biohazardous materials. In this instance, she'd found the remnants of an enthusiastic coupling, and every trace of that needed to be disposed of and decontaminated. The dead don't complain, so Mona found stripped skin behind the TV, streaks of embalming fluid on the mini-fridge and a great lake of it under the bed, and even a lubricated glass eye gazing up from the drain of the empty bathtub. Her red bucket—*Hazardous Waste* stickered on its side—is now ready to empty into the incinerator.

Third difference: Mona does her best to sanitize the place, both physically and spiritually. Disinfection and specialized cleaning methods help remove bacteria and viruses, but she's also come to believe that saying a simple prayer over the cleansed space helps erase the less-obvious stains. Mona thinks of the folks who'd set up camp outside the motel as fanatics, but a blessing can't hurt, can it?

Surveying her morning's work, Mona congratulates herself on her care. Here in the Greenlee Suite there are no more stains, streaks, crust, or smears, and the room now smells more like a citrus grove than a sperm-splattered butcher's shop.

She's about to wheel the housekeeping trolley back outside, stacked with its supplies and burdened by a wobbling front-left wheel, when a thought at the back of her mind causes her to circuit the room just one last time—and it's lucky she does.

Behind the cushion of the largest seat, Mona finds a small piece of scalp, sticky with lube and trailing a matted clump of hay-blonde hair. Sighing with relief, she collects the errant scrap, sanitizes the spot, and finally heads to the door. A second before she leaves she makes the sign of the cross with her fingers, taps her brow and heart, and heads back out into the corridor with the satisfaction of another job well done.

Motel Styx

"

My clients are concerned that this business is not only an ethical abomination, but also a public health disaster waiting to happen, and it appalls the majority of Texans. Federal laws may allow for such deviance, but this atrocity must be opposed at state level.

"

- Daphne Mackay, Civil Litigation Lawyer

Finally Alone

At the beginning of the corridor leading to Ellis' room, he and Merl walk by a machine that vends bags of ice. A simple, computer-printed sign is taped to the front. *Limit 2 Bags Per Room, Per 24-hr Period*, the black-on-white decrees.

Ellis has already had enough of Motel Styx, and tries to ignore the meaning of the full-bag ice machine and the gruesome art on the walls as they pass: framed oil paintings of idyllic countryside, each with a decaying corpse splayed somewhere in the scene, marring its tranquility.

"My brother Silas does those," Merl comments. "Not the backgrounds, mind you; he finds those at thrift stores. He adds the bodies, paints them right into the scenes like they've been lying there the whole time."

"Truly visionary," Ellis mutters, trying to regain composure after witnessing the atrocity in Yamamoto's wetroom.

"We both like adding our own touches to things. After I bought the motel, the first thing I did was design this inner hallway and move the doors of the rooms to the inside of the building. Keeps the bodies out of the heat and the gawkers to a minimum."

He stops in front of a door with a '3' on it and points to another on the other side of the hall. "Room 12 across the way is the theater. Movie and performance times are on your itinerary. Anyway, tour's over and I'm rambling. Room 3 is yours. Try your keycard."

Ellis swipes his card above the black screen on the lock and opens the door. The air smells like lemons, must, and a hint of bleach.

"Welcome to the Greenlee Suite," Merl says. "I had your luggage brought in." He points to the hardshell tucked neatly inside the door.

Ellis looks around his room—more spacious than his bedroom back home—and relief washes over him. Posing as a VIP at this hellhole may have forced him to take out a loan worth a quarter of last year's annual income, but at least it has afforded him to relax in style.

A dark gray duvet covers a king-size bed. In the middle, a basket filled with fresh fruit, condoms, a bottle of wine, and a magnum of champagne sits waiting to thank him for his patronage. A three-piece set of cherry-coloured leather furniture surrounds a TV covering most of one wall, while the cool grays and blues of the rest of the room bring to Ellis' mind the pallid flesh of corpses. That unpleasant thought vanishes when he sees a giant spa tub through the open bathroom doorway.

"The Greenlee is basically the presidential suite, so you've got it all: complimentary drinks cabinet, boosted Wi-Fi, room service at the touch of a button, and..."

"That's great. Thanks so much, Merl," Ellis says, feeling his tension re-emerge. He doesn't want more explanations in a place that doesn't make sense to him. He doesn't *want* it to make sense.

Merl continues, pointing to a framed painting above the bed. Ellis' research has told him that it's Karen Greenlee, an infamous necrophile and the namesake of the room. "Silas painted that one, too," Merl says. "She's a bit of a folk hero, ain't she? I've been trying to organize a meet-and-greet for you VIPs, but she's gone into hiding, not really a fan of the publicity. I don't think she's lost her interest in bodies though. Once a morgue rat, always a morgue rat!"

"True. Look, the room is great and you've been so accommodating, but I really would like to rest, thank you."

"Sure, of course," Merl says. "Just promise me you won't share the Jacuzzi tub with any of the bodies, okay? The drains tend to clog, and..."

"You don't need to worry about that," Ellis says, his skull starting to throb.

"And let me know if you've any problems with the room at all. The Graveyard Fantasy suite isn't booked too often if you'd like to take it instead. We got an actual hole dug in the ground with a coffin at the bottom, and a fog machine too. Or, if you like a more sterile atmosphere, there's the morgue setup available tomorrow afternoon once we clean..."

"Like I said, this is great. I find themed rooms distracting anyway."

Merl's face turns quizzical. "But you said you've been to Toronto?"

In his irritation Ellis forgot that Toronto—essentially a fun park for necrophiles—specializes in themed rooms. "Yeah, I, uh, had to specify during booking. Otherwise I'd have ended up in one of their spaceship rooms or something, and close encounters of the third kind aren't my thing!" He laughs too hard.

"Okay, well just one mor..."

"*Merl*," Ellis snaps.

The motel owner jumps to attention.

"I said, *thank you.*"

Merl turns to the door. "Okay, Mr. Macintosh. I can tell it's been a long day. You'll find your itinerary on the desk, so just shout if you need anything." He leaves with a polite click of the door.

Ellis hears himself whimper. He hates making that sound, and as he stands in the center of a motel room he can barely afford he gets that familiar dreaded feeling again: like the world is shaping him, rather than the opposite. He feels the winding path of the Styx conveyor belt moving his feet as waxed autopsy strings puppeteer his arms; there's a voice speaking in his head that isn't his own. He can't control anything, least of all here in this vile den of corpses, corpse-fuckers, and...*Emeley*.

His eyes prickle. "How could you hurt me like this, Em?" he asks.

He tugs the hardshell over to the bed, sits down, and

drags the zipper around its perimeter. After rummaging for a moment, he finds a black plastic case that rattles as he removes it. Inside, a box of three-dozen unsharpened pencils wait for use. He lays the box on the dresser, takes one pencil out, and holds it in both fists.

Snap.

His stress drops to the carpet with the two splintered pieces.

Now he can think.

He pictures Emeley on their trip to Miami, before the disappointments and the failures and the losses. She stands in the sunshine, a breeze blowing her dark hair like a kite behind her. That vacation was perfect—she didn't nag him about anything, the food and drinks were incredible, the weather was great, and they danced most nights. The sex—though he doesn't want to think of it now, in this place—was some of the best they'd ever had. The memory is a far cry from where they ended up, so how could they have gone from those seven days of bliss, to *this*? Her without him? Her with *these* people?

"You can't leave me, Em," he says firmly. "Why did you think you could?"

Ellis only ever tried to help her. That had been the shape of his love: guidance, support, and direction. When they'd met she'd been a slob and they'd shared a single dance at a stupid Tango class—chock full of too many wannabe alpha males competing for a space that was so obviously his. Despite her shortcomings, the one dance was enough to hook Ellis, enough for him to recognize that she was the sole reason he'd felt the need to attend the lesson. Fate brought them together so he could mold her into something more.

Now he's here, in a fucking *necrotel*, wondering

what the hell had gone wrong. He'd always known that Emeley was destined for better things than she thought she deserved, so he'd fed that spark of hers and watched it grow. Even with the way things ended, this will be the way he will prove how precious she had been, once and for all. While she may no longer be around in spirit, he knows she is here now, physically, or will be very soon.

Through the wall behind the desk he hears a woman laughing in the midst of what sounds like a one-sided conversation. He tries not to consider who or what she may be talking to.

Ellis returns to the contents of his luggage. He'd packed light, with only a couple of extra shirts and a second pair of pants. Beneath the clothes, he's tucked a folder full of printouts concerning the other corpse motels: FAQ pages, reviews, a printed book detailing the history of the legalized necrotel, and other scraps he'd found to help him sell his story. Under the folder, a crowbar, a near-silent drill, and a lockpicking kit sit nestled at the bottom of the case. His contact Veronika told him to purchase it all after arriving in Texas. He considers every door he's seen, secured by electronic locks, rendering the lockpicking kit useless. Why did Veronika ask him to buy it? What door is he missing?

The luggage holds something else too—a secret safety net, a last resort: carefully concealed in its lining and waiting for a reason to be used is a newly-purchased handgun. With the blessing of Texas freedom and no waiting period, he'd acquired it shortly after he'd landed at El Paso International. He'd rightly assumed that, despite Merl's "no guns on guests" policy, there would be no metal detector or formal checks—especially for a top-paying customer like Ellis.

He picks up the envelope containing Emeley's suicide note. It bears his name, handwritten in jagged lettering that suggests she was anxious and hurried when she scrawled it. Ellis takes it to the desk and leans it against the tall mirror, ignoring his nervous reflection.

His VIP package itinerary lies on the desk. Interspersed between movie showings in the theater, karaoke in the lounge, and other members-only events, three separate room service times serving him cold bodies as "companions" have been printed in bold. With a strange combination of fear and anticipation, he reads "*4pm— Your First Rendezvous.*"

Ellis checks the time on his phone—deliberately disregarding the notifications on the screen—and closes his luggage. The hour of reckoning is nearly upon him, but he doesn't feel ready to face it.

He needs whisky and to find Veronika—both of which should be in the lounge—but he's too slow to act: as he's approaching the door he hears the knock he has been dreading.

Motel Styx

"

Don't believe the nay-sayers or the lies. Motel Styx is a safe, friendly, and professional establishment for all consenting adults.

"

- Merl Bonvante, Proprietor of Motel Styx

The First Body

"Room service!" comes a voice through the wood.

A tingling like a swarm of insects rushes across Ellis' skin. Standing in the center of his fancy room, he feels his legs sway, almost buckle. He pushes aside his nerves to check his reflection in the small mirror on the wall, smooths his shirt, and prepares himself for what he's about to see: a dead body that *could* be Emeley. He'd be lucky if it was, but maybe that's not the right word. If he were lucky, she wouldn't be dead in the first place.

Arnie, the masturbating man from the behind-the-scenes tour, stands in the hallway bent over one end of a sheet-covered gurney. From what Ellis can tell, the size of the body is right for his late wife. He steps aside and lets the man wheel her in.

"She's a real pretty one," Arnie says, without making eye contact. He laughs nervously.

Ellis feels his jaw clench with distaste. Had this fucker squirted a load out over her before bringing her in?

"Thanks," Ellis says through gritted teeth.

Arnie makes no move to leave, and Ellis views him without shock for the first time: lank, chin-length hair that needs a wash, a long, pointed nose, and a pair of droop-lidded eyes hovering just south of 'dim-witted.' It's hard to avoid a mental comparison with an Igor-type horror movie character, but Ellis doubts any of those silver-screen lab assistants were ever witnessed jacking off over the experiments. He senses that a tip is appropriate, but while he wants nothing more than to pull the sheet away and see if it's his Emeley under there, he can wait; there's no way he's giving money to this skinny pervert.

Ellis had given clear specifications in his application for his VIP package, trying to increase his chances of being *given* his wife so he won't have to *take* her. While most guests who book stays at Motel Styx no doubt just list the physical attributes that most arouse them, in the hope of getting their perfect match in a cadaver, Ellis summarized his wife Emeley in a list of descriptive bullet points:

- Pretty, but not beautiful
- Dark brown hair
- Small breasts
- Small waist
- No tattoos
- Scars okay

A strand of deep brunette hair falls from beneath the cover.

It really might be her...

"I can put her on the bed if you want." Arnie points to the king-size and smiles, pulling Ellis from his reverie.

"No," Ellis replies.

Arnie frowns a moron's frown.

Ellis softens his voice. "I've got it. Just leave her."

Arnie laughs again; a boyish giggle, as though they're sharing a secret to keep from the adults. "Okay, well have fun!" he says, before bounding to the door and closing it behind him.

When Ellis approaches the shrouded body, he's surprised to find that, nestled amidst his nervousness, there's an undeniable excitement. He feels like a chef about to unveil a great feast. Can it be her? Had Merl accepted his wife into the collection and just asked his lackeys to add a lick or two of makeup to conceal her blemishes? He sniffs the air, trying to catch the familiar scent of his late partner, but all he smells is a faint whiff of that herbaceous gift shop candle, formaldehyde, clinging to the space around it.

In a single pull, he removes the white covering. His hope crumples on the floor with it.

A nude stranger lies beneath.

The hair is a shade too dark; not 'mocha,' as Emeley always called her own. The jawline, too soft. The nose, too narrow. The eyes, no doubt polished glass, stare unnaturally upward; vibrant stars in a cold dead sky.

Ellis backsteps to the bed and sits down, crushed and unsettled to be alone with the naked corpse of someone he doesn't know. Behind the one-way glass, the sun begins to set and the warm glow of early evening settles over the room. He imagines the alien woman defrosting in the rays to the point of melting away, but the beams weaken and she does nothing to dematerialize.

He glugs down a small bottle of vodka from the mini fridge and looks at his phone again. The unread messages he's been ignoring are from Damien, his wife's twin brother. Her goddamn male doppelganger.

Only guilty people run, Ellis

And:

This is all going to finally catch up with you

And:

I'm about thirty seconds away from calling my lawyer

He takes two more pencils from the case and breaks them, one by one.
Snap.
Breathe.
Snap!
He returns to the gurney. Arnie was right, the woman had been a stunner. She looks to have died in her 20s, when youth was on her side. Despite his initial unease, the corpse's glass eyes give her a blank but peaceful look. Ellis can almost imagine that she's still alive, roused from a dream and about to take her first waking breath. Her hair is nearer to an umber brown and it frames her frozen face in two glossy waves. Her plump lips appear—Ellis hates to think it—*sensual*, in a way that Emeley's never were. The tits are much larger than Emeley's, and the face

too close to a conventional beauty. No scar above her brow, no scars anywhere.

He can't help but picture what this pristine dead woman might have looked like when she was still breathing, with something long and hard thrust into her mouth...

"Shit man, get a grip," he says.

It's not a 'her', he remembers. It's an 'it'.

Like Emeley.

No, not like Emeley. She's different.

He turns away and Karen Greenlee stares down at him from her portrait above the bed. The painted lines of her face make her look weak and impulsive and it irritates Ellis that she'd so easily stolen a corpse, right from its own funeral, when he can barely look at one.

On the gurney, the dead woman's skin is cold and gray. He pokes a thigh. It sinks, then slowly returns to its former position, a rubbery texture so different to a living being. He gropes one of its breasts—a cool, meaty handful—and is glad when it does nothing for him. Glad, but terribly morose.

"See? I can touch her, you sick bitch," he says, glaring at Karen Greenlee on the wall. "I just think it's wrong."

The sadness in his chest inflates into anger and he stands above the cadaver, hating her for not being his wife... his love... *his.* He grabs the sheet from the floor and throws it in a large clump atop the woman's face and upper body.

The neighbor's solitary voice drifts through the wall again, muffled but affectionate.

Another message comes through on his phone. This one from Veronika.

Rumor has it you're in the building. When do we meet?

Ellis slides past the gurney, pulls open the door to his room, hangs the placard that reads 'Do Not Disturb, Dead Busy' —ha *fucking* ha—on the hallway-side doorknob, and paces to the bar.

Top notch Scotch

If I wasn't here for the bodies, I'd come for the booze

Members Lounge

His keycard chirps and the small light on the black box changes from red to green. The door pushes into a cozy, dark room lit only by neon-tube beer logos and string lights tacked around the perimeter.

The first section of the Members Lounge is laid out like a cozy café, with two bookshelves filled with a range of morbid tomes and a tall shelving stack of board games. On a small table, an altered version of *Guess Who?* lies abandoned mid-game. In both a copyright and taste infringement, someone has replaced the faces with criminals. Among others he doesn't recognize, Ted Bundy, Jeffrey Dahmer, and Dennis Nilsen sit grinning, their identifying features waiting to be described by a player, but their unibrows and ugly glasses are nowhere near as memorable as their horrible actions. *Does your guy have a barrel full of body parts in his bedroom?*

At the first book shelf, he skim-reads a few of the fiction titles, signed by their twisted authors and marked up to exorbitant prices. Spines that read *Dead Inside*,

NecroSutra, *Toxic Love*, *Necrophilia Variations*, and *Exquisite Corpse* sit beside one another. A duo have even written a book about the motel itself, titled *Motel Styx* which, judging by its synopsis, is little more than exploitative trash.

More framed images of corpses—some being enjoyed by living men and women—adorn the walls. Ignoring their finer details, Ellis heads further inside and when the lights dip to a more intimate level he takes one of the five stools at the L-shaped bar. Though busy, the bar feels quieter than one in an average hotel.

A woman with pixie-cut black hair comes out through a back door behind the bar. The combination of her faux-leather apron and a network of tribal tattoos across her arms makes him imagine her as a *Game of Thrones* extra. She's shorter than her Instagram photos led him to believe and at least ten years Ellis' junior, but he finds some comfort in her familiar face. And though her bold look is something he generally finds distasteful, he still feels an attraction to her. She makes eye contact and he gives her a small smile, one strangers might give in passing, and one that wouldn't suggest they'd been talking for hours planning a body heist.

"Hello, Veronika."

"Ah ah," she says and waves a finger in dissuasion, then points to the nametag pinned to her apron. It reads *Dani*.

"Hello, Dani," Ellis corrects.

"You made it."

He shrugs. "The mini bar wasn't cutting it."

"The motel is a long way to come for a drink of any kind." She grins. Her feline eyes pop out of her face, making Ellis warily think of a cat watching a mouse. "Let the

76

games begin."

He hopes that what he sees in her expression is her excitement for their plan, but when she props her elbows onto the bar in front of him and focuses those huge green eyes onto him, he senses a recklessness in her.

"Did you bring the fake ID?" she asks, raising her brows like she's about to receive a gift.

"Merl said he didn't need my identification. Not for the price I'm paying."

She laughs, rising from the bar again. "You don't need one. I just wanted to see if you would get one."

"What the hell?" he blurts. "Do you know how much I paid for that?"

Still chuckling, she puts out her hand, palm up. "I can't...*won't* serve you until you show me."

Irritated by this introduction to his sole contact at the motel, he yanks the fake ID from his wallet and slaps it onto the bar. The dim light does nothing to hide its poor printing and lamination. Even though Veronika knows who he really is, his heart still pounds under the scrutiny—memories of being a teen trying to get into clubs flood his mind as a warmth floods his cheeks.

"Going undercover using your real first name is a bold choice," she says.

"I thought it was clever."

"It's a pretty good forgery otherwise." She hands it back to him.

"It really isn't."

She winks. "Most of the people coming here use an alias. What'll it be, then?"

"On the house, I hope, after this trouble." He holds up the fake ID he doesn't need.

"Sure."

"Bourbon. Some coke, too."

She disappears once Ellis has his drink. He shakes his head and sips.

Gonna need to keep that one in line.

He checks his phone for the time, as though the body in his room might disappear if he waits long enough. His nerves are fried. The body isn't Emeley, so will they be able to tell he hasn't...*used* the merchandise? Will they call him out? Surely not—especially with Merl's policies regarding contraceptives and privacy.

Veronika appears again and Ellis tries to catch her eye, but before he can spark a conversation she cries, "Hey there! What can I get you, hun?"

A man, roughly Ellis' same height but bulkier in build, leans on the bar beside him. "Gimme a coffee..." He stops to read her name tag. "...*Dani.*"

Clearly another staff member, he wears a white shirt and keeps his hair scruffy. The man gives off a brooding, predatory air as he watches the bartender make his drink, popping the joints in his arms and hands as though limbering up for a fight. The tough-guy posturing sickens Ellis. He can tell by looking at the man that he probably drops his weights at the gym too.

The man turns and seems to recognize him. "*Wellllll*, Mr. Macintosh. I'm Chris, Head of Security. How are you enjoying your stay so far?"

Ellis clears his throat. "I'm good. It's...good. But how did you..."

"It's my job to know. How else can I look after the VIPs and deliver the star treatment?" Chris dips into a slight bow.

Veronika serves him an espresso and watches, amused.

Ellis bristles. "There's no need for that."

Chris straightens up. "At this fine establishment we beg to differ—especially for necs like you, with such a genteel constitution."

"What do you mean?"

"Heard you weren't a fan of my man Yamamoto's little show. Heard you nearly lost your lunch!" Chris explodes into laughter and claps Ellis' back.

Ellis manages to avoid scowling. "We aren't all like him, you know. Some of us are here for other reasons."

"Like what—*love?*" Chris asks, and flutters his lashes. "You won't find much of that here, just humping. But there's no need to be squeamish, Mac—we're all friends, and we all prefer our partners cold and quiet. The only difference is that folks like Yamamoto like to cut 'em as well as to fuck 'em."

Ellis takes a mouthful of his drink. "Does Merl know you speak to the clients this way?"

Chris raises his hands, as if to prove he means no harm. "Hey, hey, I'm just security. I'm not trained in customer service. I don't mean any offense."

"Some star treatment."

Veronika offers a sly smile. "You know, Ellis, you should be grateful he's around."

"Why's that?"

"Well, we aren't *all* friends."

"*Hey*," Chris warns, raising his eyebrows at her, but she continues.

"Class 9 necs are always a threat, even inside the motel." Her voice trembles, like she's telling a ghost story. "Before places like Motel Styx opened up, I've heard something like 40 percent of documented necs resorted to murder to get the bodies they craved. Look around the room."

Ellis swivels on his stool and glances at the small crowd.

Veronika continues: "If it's true, almost half of everyone in here is a killer. *You* might be a killer, Ellis. *Are* you a killer?"

He rotates his stool back to face her, his ears warming again. "No."

"Well, Yama—"

"Stop!" Chris points an angry finger Veronika's way, wafting out tobacco and motor oil. "That's enough!"

"I'm only having a little fun."

"Merl won't like you spreading lies. Knock it off." He huffs. "And quoting stats like that ain't fair. 'Documented' don't mean shit—what about all the cases nobody knows about? The EMTs, the crime scene folks, the nurses?"

Veronika reaches across the counter and prods one of Chris' shoulders. "You're getting a bit upset. Maybe you should go take your bike for a ride and cool down."

Ellis feels an unpleasant recognition run through him. "You...you ran a ring around those protesters when I arrived, didn't you? Blew up the dust and forced them closer to the car?"

Chris grins. "Didn't realize it was you out there, Mac." He slugs his coffee.

Ellis stares, forcing himself to meet the man's eye. "You're security, it's your job to know, remember?"

Chris leans in close to Ellis, their noses almost touching. "I just saw a bunch of assholes and gave 'em what they deserve."

"Get out, Chris," Veronika demands. "Stop fucking with him."

"You started it," Chris says, shaking his head and grinning.

Veronika maintains a hard stare and to Ellis' surprise the Head of Security raises his hands in appeasement and struts back out of the bar, still sniggering.

"You can't let him get to you," Veronika says. "His ego is bigger than his dick *and* his gun for that matter."

Ellis lowers his voice. "I just want to find my wife."

Her eyes sparkle. "Well, I've got some good news for you: she's here, Ellis." She puts another drink in front of him. "Came in on the afternoon delivery."

Ellis sits up. "Then what are we doing? I could have her and be gone by now!"

"*Lower your voice,*" she hisses. "You can't do anything without me, and right now I'm on the clock."

Ellis is growing tired of the way she speaks to him, but before he can put her back in her place a thin young guy with an acne-riddled jawline and a backwards baseball cap approaches the bar to order. The man doesn't flirt with Veronika and, though she smiles as she passes him a tray of drinks, her eyes are as glassy as those of the dead woman back in Ellis' room. The capped man crosses the bar and sits alone at a booth.

In the next booth over, three bros talk and laugh in reserved tones despite already clearly being several-drinks-deep. Words escape the secrecy of the table's conversation—'tits', 'slut', 'bitch', 'pussy'—and Ellis realizes they've bonded over their shared love of fucking women who can't say no. A trio of misogynists living out their aggressive fantasies in the only legal way possible. He doubts *they'd* flirt with a woman like Veronika either, but they might try to fuck his dead wife. With her here, they might get the chance.

Across from the bros, a slender but toned dark-skinned woman in a low-cut dress sits reading a worn paperback of *Le Nécrophile*. She lowers the book to sip her beer and with a shock, Ellis notices Yamamoto beyond her at the far side of the room, nursing what appears to be a tomato juice. Their eyes meet and Yamamoto dips his head, wearing the ghost of a grin.

"He likes it because it looks like blood," Veronika says, returning to a place in front of Ellis as she polishes a glass. "Aren't you due a guest?"

"Hmmm?" Ellis asks, turning back to her.

She leans in and whispers, "VIPs don't usually spend much time in here because Merl spoils them. You need to play the part, Ellis. Keep up appearances."

"Ah, yeah. I had one, but my neighbor wouldn't shut up. Bit of a mood killer."

Veronika nods knowingly, pleased with his reply. "Then, you could use another drink."

"Yes, please."

"I think you're next to Linette. If you haven't met her, I'm sure you will soon."

"Does she ever quiet down?"

"Talking is kinda her thing, but you can't worry about distractions or performance anxiety." She raises her voice for the second half of her reply, making eye contact with others in the lounge: "Don't feel bad. Most guys get it at some point."

Her playful demeanor is starting to piss Ellis off. He's never had trouble performing, and for her to suggest it makes him want to show her just how well he can fuck.

Veronika hands him a sheet with better lamination than his fake ID, and the promise of another drink calms him. The cocktails—with names like *Skull Fucker*, *Grave-tini*, and *Corpse-mopolitan*—seem geared more toward the tourists that aren't allowed in the Members Lounge.

"They're a bit silly, aren't they?" Veronika says. "Merl loves leaning into the theme."

"Yeah, I saw the gift shop. I can't believe I'm saying this, but I'll have a *Rotting Man-hattan*." Ellis sticks out his tongue and points a finger in his mouth like he's gagging.

Veronika furrows her brow and the stern face looks cute on her. "Are you yucking someone's yum?" she asks, pulling a cocktail shaker from its home behind the bar.

"As you know, I prefer them fresher," Ellis says, to be sure she remembers he isn't interested in sex with the dead. "Like, a lot fresher. Still warm."

"To each their own. We host all kinds here." Veronika points to the woman reading the book and whispers: "That's Ruth. I call her Ruthless. She fucks bones."

The woman looks so normal to Ellis; a bohemian-type he'd see at a café back in New York, reading something for a psychology class, coyly satisfied by a humble vibrator behind closed doors.

Ellis moves the conversation back to the bartender. "What's your type then?" he asks, with a practiced smile. He'd never gone out searching for women, but there were times when they found him more than willing, even when he was already taken. Emeley had her suspicions about his infidelities, but he was too smart to get caught. Now she's gone and it doesn't matter *what* Ellis gets up to anymore. Maybe a good, hard fuck is what he needs.

"God, I haven't been asked 'my type' since I worked at a roadside joint up in Valentine," Veronika says.

"That where you're from?"

"Yeah. I took this job to get away from it. I feel more like 'me' working here—plus I get to flex my creative muscles whenever a client wants their rendezvous in makeup."

Ellis notices the elaborate flick of her eyeliner, the sleek brows, the metallic purple of her lids, and the subtle peach lipstick.

"Bartender, secret informer, *and* makeup artist?" Ellis asks.

"Sure, and more. A Jill-of-all-trades." She plays with the badge hanging from a lanyard around her neck.

A Jill-of-all-trades with an all-access pass.

"To be honest, I *love* working here," she says, with a suggestive kink in her lips.

"Oh," Ellis says, catching the implication. He tries to make his distaste sound like surprise. "So you're...you're one too. You didn't tell me that online."

"I figured you'd assume. You can say it, by the way, *necrophile*—it's not a dirty word. But I'm more like the ultimate pansexual."

"What does that mean?"

"I don't discriminate. I'm a slut for it all. All colors, all creeds. Male, female, or other. Tight and alive, deceased and falling off the bone. It's all yum in my book." She leans forward as she lowers the *Rotting Man-hattan* onto a coaster in front of Ellis. Despite the way her words revolt him, his eyes have another appetite as he gazes at the swell of her cleavage packed into the tight, sleeveless black top behind her apron.

"I can't be the only living guest that's ever hit on you," Ellis says with a wink.

Veronika smirks. "Not the first married one either.

What *will* your wife think?" She nods toward the wedding band on Ellis' left hand.

Ellis' mood drops. *The bitch knows she's dead, knows she's in a bag somewhere on the premises.* "Don't."

"Why'd you wear the ring, Ellis?"

"I didn't really think about it."

"Same name, same ring. You aren't trying very hard to hide who you are, or why you're here."

Ellis grows tired of her bullshit. "You said you'd help me. When are you going to do that?"

"We have an agreement."

"Then when are you off tonight..." He looks down at her nametag. "...*Dani*? Or whatever your name is."

She laughs, then opens a plastic box behind the bar and shows him a small collection of nametags, each one bearing a different moniker.

She's crazy, this one. Her hair may be black, but she reminds Ellis of some pink-and-green-haired, personality-disorder-pussy he'd tasted in the past. Fun, but a hell of a liability if she's in the wrong mood—or when Ellis is.

"Who *are* you then?" he asks.

"Just like the bodies, I can be whoever you want." She raises her eyebrows and rummages in the names, like a bingo caller digging for the next numbered ball, then takes out her hand to touch his wedding ring. "I could be *her*."

Ellis shakes his head and speaks through gritted teeth. "I doubt you'd have it in there."

The bartender lifts a label machine from beneath the bar and drops it like a rock on the bartop in front of him, sending a ripple over the top of his drink.

"It has an unconventional spelling, doesn't it?" she asks.

Ellis' mind swims as Veronika types on the small keyboard. "What's wrong with you?"

The bartender hits the print button on the machine.

C H E R R I E S the label reads.

"I'm sorry!" Veronika laughs. "I'm relabeling the garnish station! You really thought I was going to type her name?"

"What I really think is that I need to get drunk."

Ellis downs several of the bar's distastefully named drinks, forsaking the diet he usually keeps to impress the clients he helps keep in shape. He watches Veronika as she tends to the other members, imagining her mouth on his body, responding to his hands in the ways that the corpse in his room and his dead wife cannot. He could stare at her all night, this conceited tease, thinking of the ways he'll make her pay for fucking him around, and the more he drinks, the more keen he becomes.

A meek-looking man in glasses, having finished the drink he'd been nursing, stands up from a small table near the entrance.

Just as Ellis notices the impact the alcohol is having on him, Veronika nods toward the guy as he leaves. In a suggestive voice, she says, "*That* one. He comes in for hot toddies to clear his nose, because he gets off on the smell of death."

"

We're all fascinated by death. That's natural. What ISN'T natural is sticking your dick in it.

"

- @StopItCarl1972, X (formally Twitter)

Interlude:

Room 9 — The Sniffer

Eric walks back to his room, his olfactory system alert to the scents of the motel around him: the musty hallway rug overdue for a vacuum, the sharp tang of bleach sneaking out under the crack of the door leading to the prep areas, and the pickly odor that already has his blood moving southerly: *formalin*. He sniffs and follows the trail like a bloodhound, delighting as it grows stronger.

In his other life, the one where he pretends to have normal interests—bowling, antiquing, and fishing—his nose pays his bills. The Lead Odor Tester for a personal hygiene company, he spends his working hours sniffing acceptable household scents and their variations, suggesting changes to the formulas to reach the desired final product that will appease the masses.

For a man with such a unique nose whose days consist of testing socially acceptable odors, it makes sense that those pleasant smells have come to bore him.

Eric doesn't want any more cut grass or fresh linen.

He doesn't want mandarin or lavender, lemon or roses.

He prefers the overworn shoes and greasy balls at the bowling lanes; the musty and smoke-damaged furniture at the antiques malls; the stink of the bait and the insides of the fish he catches; the pissed-on alleyway walls and the shat-upon sidewalks. And when even these nauseating fumes are no longer enough, he books a room at this motel in the desert to find the basest, most disgusting scents in the world.

Before he opens the door to his room, he removes a black velvet eye mask from his pocket and stretches its elastic band around his head. It doesn't matter what the body looks like, who it was, or what's between its legs.

The only thing that matters is how it smells.

The man presses the door closed behind him and reaches his arms out into the room. Following a straight path to the end of the bed, his fingers find the edge of a body bag, then the zipper running the length of the polymer. Its thick plastic scent briefly rises to his nose before the aromas he has paid to inhale plume out and replace it.

The open bag releases cadaverine and putrescine; the intoxicating perfumes of death. He pushes down on the body's belly until pungent gasses shoot from its lips and asshole and into his talented nose, causing him to gag on a liquid rush of nausea before inhaling even more deeply. Into his mouth and nostrils climbs the fecal fetor of skatole, alongside hints of tallow and hyacinth, and the rotten-egg reek of hydrogen sulfide. The man shifts the body, the oozing skin malleable in his grip, then shoves his face into its pits and crevices, seeking out the mothball malodour of indole, quick moments of asphalt and urine, and the cabbagey stink of methanethiol.

The stench is suffocating, overwhelming, and Eric has done well to avoid vomiting yet. It will soon be inevitable. Sometimes, all it takes is a waft; other times a foul expulsion of human gasses are needed to push him past the brink of tolerance.

Eric undresses, the mask still blinding him but his scent organ guiding the way. Tugging the zipper all the way down, he clambers into the bag beside the body and smothers himself in the heavy bouquet of hundreds of chemicals hard at work, creating the perfect haze of his favorite drug, the concoction that moves him to ecstasy.

With one hand he pumps at his groin.

With the other, he pulls the zip closed, sealing them both in the bag, where he nuzzles his moldering companion in the dark.

Motel Styx

Hell on Earth!

No stars. No review. I'll let God speak for me instead:
"But the cowardly, the unbelieving, the vile, the
murderers, the sexually immoral, those who practice magic
arts, the idolaters and all liars—their place will be in the
fiery lake of burning sulfur. This is the second death."
- Revelations 21:8

Three's a Crowd

Ellis thought this was what he needed: some drinks, some chatter, and a woman with a pulse, but as he and the bartender head back to his room, her ass on full display in a pair of tight pleather pants, the reality of the situation comes crashing down around him. Veronika is in control and he is drunkenly returning to a room with a corpse in it, accompanied by a necrophile.

He'd tried to convince her to end her shift early. Tried to stop her pouring him so many goddamned whiskies. But she had a way about her; a flirting, assertive way.

He throws open the door and it hits the gurney still parked inside.

"Don't mind herrr," Ellis says as he stumbles in, hoping he can keep all his drinks down and straighten out his thoughts.

"We've talked all night, and you never once said you *still* had the body in your room!" Veronika cries, her voice clear and bright, sober.

"Surprissse," Ellis says, without enthusiasm.

"This is like a beer left out to warm! You should crack them while they're cold! Major party foul!"

Her words throw Ellis into further disarray.

"Have you ever had a threesome?" Veronika asks, standing at the trolley's side to peek beneath the crumpled sheet he'd dumped atop the body.

Ellis wants to sound experienced, fun, but his heart is pounding and the alcohol has turned to mulch in his belly. "Surrrre. Of courssse." The truth is that he'd suggested a three-way to Emeley a couple of times, but she never went for it. "Lookkk, are we gon get Emly?"

"We don't need her when we've already got this beauty right here." She scoops up the jumble of linen and tosses it into a corner of the room.

"That's not..." Ellis slurs. "You sai...you said she's here an thas wat we were waiting for."

"Wow. She's got great tits," Veronika says, transfixed by the dead woman.

He thinks back to the momentary groping he'd braved. "They're okkkayyy. Prefer yoursss." Ellis goes to the bed, sits down, and lazily pats the space beside him, hoping to draw her away from the silent third party.

"You okay?" Veronika asks.

"Jusss drunk. Come here. Let's talk about the plaaan."

She steps closer but stops at the phone, dials a number, and says, "Can we get a Pummel Horse? Yeah, the

Greenlee Suite."

"The *hell* is a Pummel Horse?"

"It's part of the plan!"

Ellis' inebriated brain pictures a battering ram, a powerful tool to bust through every door between him and his wife. "Is it gonna helllpp?"

Veronika opens the drawer of the bedside table and removes a book that she throws onto the bed next to Ellis. Instead of a bible—what he'd expect to find in a motel room drawer—it's a thin catalog labeled 'Apparatus and Costume'.

French maid, fireman, and animal outfits remind him of a cheap costume and display store.

"Disssguises?"

Veronika laughs.

He skims through it, eyes wide with surprise and disgust. Sex toys and body props fill the remainder of the pages. A golden object shaped like a cock, called 'Osiris' Penis', is described as simulating an erection, allowing the user to ride a cadaver in cowgirl.

"Page five."

Through swimming vision, Ellis finds the page, but he can't read the description beneath the wood and padded leather build.

"I don underssssstand."

"It's for her," Veronika says, and points to the corpse. "How drunk are you? I mean, I know exactly how drunk you are because I made the drinks, but..."

The thought of doing anything with the body on the gurney, even moving it onto this sex mount, nauseates him. A surge of unpleasant ideas sluices through his head, breaking through the alcohol-induced fog. It feels worse than simple disgust: it all goes entirely against nature.

"Emly iss here, you *fucking* sssaid!"

"I did say, but I was wrong. She hasn't arrived yet. Now focus! Do you know how many guests would love an opportunity like this? One living, one dead?" Veronika stalks the room, full of confidence, keeping her eyes on Ellis as she positions herself behind the cadaver's head. She runs her hands beneath its heavy breasts, cupping them.

Ellis doesn't want to be here anymore. He wants to check out, leave the state, leave the country. He can't get far enough away from this hell. But...

But Emeley.

Yes, Emeley. He simply cannot leave her at the mercy of this place.

"Is everything okay? You still distracted from earlier? Linette's gone quiet. Now it's just you, me..." She motions to the corpse. "... and her."

Watching Ellis, Veronika pulls her top and bra up over her head in a single, fluid motion. Her tits are a fraction larger than the dead woman's, their nipples small but prominent. She leans forward and strokes the flesh of one of her own breasts across the cadaver's mouth, then pries the motionless thing's lips open to feed it her nipple. She wiggles it and smiles from the sensation. It's a surreal, sickening sight, but Ellis can't look away.

"So you *are* a little curious," Veronika says.

There's a knock on the door.

The bartender giggles and makes no move to cover up.

Glad for the distraction, Ellis gets up to open the door a crack and meets the sight of a man who looks like Merl—his brother Silas?—holding a device on wheels.

True to the image in the catalog, it resembles a pommel horse from his old gym classes, but with the top handles removed.

"Your Pummel Horse," the man says.

Dazed and deeply wanting to reject the delivery, Ellis instead watches himself hand the man a couple of bills.

The guy smiles and heads back down the corridor.

Ellis wheels the device inside.

Veronika has slipped two fingers into the corpse's mouth and is wriggling them against the slack tongue. "It's dry in there," she says. "But I can help with that."

Keeping her digits pushed between the body's teeth, Veronika leans over and drools a rivulet through the gap. When she stands back up she pushes her fingers in and out of its jaws with a moist slithering sound. "Much better."

The body takes what it's given. Obedient.

Ellis hates how the scene tightens his throat in revulsion but also calls involuntary warmth to his groin. He won't believe that it has anything to do with the body. It's the way Veronika is looking at him, wide-eyed and taunting.

"That's the most versatile of all the toys, here at Motel Styx," Veronika says, removing her wet fingers to point at the Pummel Horse. "They can keep their *Cruci-fucks* and the *Sex Noose*—just gimme something to prop up this beautiful girl."

"Loohhhk, we can't," Ellis slurs, all thoughts of the original plan evaporating.

Ellis only held a loose idea for retrieving Emeley, formed from the many chats online with Veronika, and a general concept of how it would go: the bartender would give Ellis her keycard while she was having a meal in the break room, so he could then access the fridge where they keep their stock of corpses, where Emeley might be lying. A half-hour to unzip body bags while Veronika keeps a lookout to distract any staff coming into the back area of the motel. Ellis and Emeley would leave via the large receiving door and carve a circular path around the building to his car. He doesn't know after that. He just wants her away from these creeps.

On Veronika's break, instead of them rushing off to rescue his wife, he'd watched her drink as many cocktails as he had throughout the evening, but in half the time. Then she'd worked the rest of her shift before dragging him back to his room where she now stands, eerily sober, molesting Ellis' first lifeless guest.

"Stohhhp, pleassse."

"*You* stop, Ellis," Veronika says. "I'm putting my ass on the line to help you, so we're doing things my way."

Ellis falters. "Isss Emly here or not?"

"Doubt it. It all takes a while to process..."

"It's been ten fucccking daysss!"

"You're drunk as hell anyway. Do you plan on driving off into the sunset like *that*?"

This bitch...

"I can handle myssssself."

"Like you can handle your finances?" she says, with a sharp edge to her voice. "No one splurges on a VIP package like this unless they want to make their visit special or they're rich—and, no offense, you don't dress like you are. Maybe they've never fucked a corpse before, but they've always fantasized, so they wanna pop their post-mortem cherry in style, but we both know that's not you. You're just desperate. You're going broke to play pretend, and I'm your only route to your wife. So you need to do as I say, and sober up for when the time comes."

Indignant, Ellis says, "Maybe you ssshould leave then. Lemme sleeeep this off."

"No," she says.

He hates that word, especially from the lips of a woman.

"You want access to Emeley? Then we're going to have some fun and you're going to *earn* my keycard."

Her tone sobers him. "Earn it? I paid you! Thisss wasn't what we agreed!"

"You paid me half."

He stares at her but she stares him down. Despite his drunkenness, he sees that she has him right where she wants him, and he fucking hates it.

Veronika saunters away from the body and into his unsteady arms, pressing her breasts against him. When she looks up with her teasing, tempting eyes, he's filled with such a bubbling rush of arousal, anger, regret, and bewilderment that he grabs the back of her pixie hair and holds her firmly, aggressively. He's here to find Emeley, but now he's going to—what? Fuck a degenerate in order to reach his wife? And why does it only feel like cheating now that she's dead?

"We both know Emeley isn't going anywhere." Veronika shuts her eyes and her lips form a lazy smile. "You can do whatever you want to me." Then, in a faint whisper: "*To us.*"

Shaking with lust and rage, Ellis wraps his hands around her throat and squeezes.

"

Whenever a shady business becomes a legal operation, it attracts dubious parties. Look at Amsterdam. Look at Bangkok. Now keep watching in the Chihuahuan Desert, 20 miles south of Valentine, Texas.

"

- Jerry Morgan, *The Blah*

The Fridge

Ellis didn't fuck the corpse.

He did *not* fuck the corpse.

Lying on his back in the dark, he listens to the bartender snore beside him.

Across the room, his other guest is still draped over the Pummel Horse, still and quiet in her eternal slumber. The scent of chemicals and body fluids that wafted from their three bodies as he and Veronika fucked still lingers in his nose. Ellis focused on Veronika's drenched pussy and the marks he'd been making on her body, while the bartender's focus was the responseless corpse, gazing at it regardless of the position Ellis had fucked her in. At one point when he'd been behind her she'd pulled away and crawled down from the bed to the dead woman. Ellis watched, panting, stinking of her, as she'd hauled the cadaver up and draped it over the Pummel Horse, before licking its face with a hunger Ellis found disturbing. He was still hard and the room was spinning when Veronika went to the body's dangling legs and rubbed her clit against its cool calves.

Angered by her stopping mid-fuck, Ellis dragged her back to the bed, choking and biting her as he thrust back into her. She smiled with reddened cheeks, spat onto his chest, then slithered down his body to take him in her mouth. He slapped her while she went down on him, and though he wished it felt to her more like a punishment, she'd loved it.

Ellis had always been into rough play and while the cadaver disgusted him, the sex was a good stress relief and nothing to feel bad about. People do far worse things when they're grieving, and after all, he *hadn't* fucked the corpse.

He should have known better than to trust some random person on the internet though, but he is here now and his lousy contact has been asleep for a while. He takes his chance, rising from the bed and padding across the floor to Veronika's discarded pleather pants. Her snorted breathing continues, a shocking contrast to the silent cadaver in the corner. In the blackness he finds them from memory, feels around in the pockets, and collects the keycard promised to him, the access he'd paid for.

Pulling on yesterday's clothes, Ellis eases the door open and creeps out into the dark and empty hall. The lights—on a motion-activated system this late at night—

pop to life as he moves towards the corridor junction. He weaves between room service trays, used body props, and soiled and discarded costumes, as occasional unreturned moans slip beneath the doors of some of the other rooms.

It must be late, considering the fact that earlier, he and Veronika had left the bar an hour after it closed, fucked in his room for a while, and then she'd passed out. With the other guests asleep or otherwise occupied, Ellis gains confidence in his still-drunken solitude. However, he knows that by stealing the bartender's keycard he's crossed a line, a big one, and perhaps the first of many.

As he walks he wonders what kind of guy Merl really is. The necrotel business has become legitimate, sure, but considering its newly legalized status, is it riddled with links to crime like the porn industry of the 80s and 90s? Or is corpse-fucking still too damn niche for the mob to bother? Merl Bonvante: passionate nec forming a company out of what he loves, or shady crook who will bury a few bodies for a business based around sex with them?

Ellis pauses at the one-way glass doorway to reception—supposedly manned 24/7, but which appears empty at the moment. He looks in on the silent gift shop, its trinkets illuminated by dim security lighting, then turns around in the vestibule and moves toward the door marked *Staff Only*, glancing once more at the abandoned lobby desk behind him before pushing his way into the restricted area.

One less barrier between him and Emeley.

The new corridor stretches into the distance, past the rooms Merl had shown him during the tour: staff lounge, prop storage, and supplies closet. Ellis jumps when, activated just like the regular hallways by his movement, the lights flicker on. At the far end, he faces the secure door. Just beyond it is the giant refrigerator and storage place of all Motel Styx's available corpses. The pantry, as Merl calls it.

With the lights now giving away his presence to anyone who happens to enter this staff-only area, Ellis raises the bartender's keycard to the black electronic lock.

"I don't know why you're back here," a deep, amused voice says.

"Shit!" Ellis spits, jumping for the second time in as many minutes.

Chris, Head of Security, marches towards him from the reception end of the corridor, carrying a pile of clothes topped with a peaked hat. "Your card won't work on that door, no matter how many times you try it."

Ellis pulls the bartender's keycard down and out of view. The door lock stays red.

Chris nears him, looking pissed. "Or did you steal a card off a staff member? No need to tell me who. Veronika gets pretty careless."

Ellis deliberately sways as he turns. "I, uh, I've had a bit to drink. Lost my way." He leans in towards Chris and exhales, hoping the security guard catches the alcohol on his breath.

"You smell more like pussy than booze to me, bud," Chris says. "But I suppose you're gonna claim you thought this was your room? Or that you needed something from your car?"

"Er...yeah. I thought this was the way out."

A dark smile grows on Chris' face. "It's *one* way out."

"Sorry. Where, uh, is my room then? Uh, my car?"

Chris puffs out his chest and crosses his arms, which are thicker than Ellis remembers, and the smile drains from his face. "Well which is it? You should pick one lie and stick to it."

Ellis takes an unconscious step back.

"What are you doing here, Mac?" Chris asks, turning gruff. "At Motel Styx."

Ellis is speechless.

"I've been in this job way too long: I know when a guest is up to something. I was just playing with you in the bar earlier—a little friendly banter—but seeing as you went green when you saw Yamamoto doing his thing today, and now I find you taking a late-night trip into an off-limits section of the motel, I'm starting to get bad feelings."

"Look, I'm no..."

"Don't start," Chris say. "You don't know who you're fucking with."

Ellis could dig his heels in and stand by his drunken cover story, but Chris looks ready to punch something, mainly Ellis' face.

"You a journalist?" Chris asks.

"No."

Chris clicks his tongue. "Cop?"

"No."

"If you're some crazy Christian on a suicide mission, I swear to fuck..."

"I'm not. I'm just a guest," Ellis says, afraid that he's about to be knocked out by this meathead. "I was just... curious. I'm sorry."

Chris extends a muscly arm.

Ellis flinches.

The raised limb merely points back down the corridor the way they'd both come. "Dry rooms are back there, as I'm sure you already know. Best you head back to yours."

"Thanks."

As Ellis passes, Chris adds, "I'm watching you, Mac."

A life saver

Finally somewhere I can be myself.

Linette

It must be nearing three in the morning by the time Ellis returns to the corridor leading to his room, where he finds an older woman wearing a fluffy lilac robe struggling at the ice machine. The spectacles hanging around her neck and the slight curve of her back remind him of his late mother.

Before the woman notices him she hefts two full bags into her arms, groaning and wobbling on her feet. "You awkward old coot," she mutters, then turns Ellis' way. Her eyes widen and she adjusts her feathered gray hair self-consciously, puts on a pair of round glasses, and says, "You startled me, young man. Would you lend a hand here, please?"

Ellis recognizes her voice as the one that carried through the wall from the room next door to his own.

She tries to hold up the two heavy bags like a child lifting freshly caught fish. When the weight is too much, she places them into Ellis' arms. "I'm Linette," she says.

"Ellis."

Linette nods at the ice. "The more we get, the longer I can spend with my Alfred."

Ellis points at the sign limiting bags. "You aren't worried about that?"

She laughs. "Pssshhhh. I'm the only one who uses these anyway. Merl doesn't mind."

"I can carry more than this, then."

"Oh, thank you!"

Ellis heaves four more bags out of the machine and follows Linette to her door, marked 2. The coolness of the ice helps clear his head. He pauses, thinking of the stolen keycard in his pocket. If Veronika wakes, decides to leave, and sees it's missing... "If you have enough, I've got to get back to my room."

Linette seems offended. "I *insist* you come and meet my husband! He'll be so grateful you helped, seeing as he can't anymore." She opens the door, gesturing with a swirl of her hand, uncannily similar to one of his mother's old mannerisms.

Haunted by the reminders, Ellis enters the low-lit room. He immediately sees the body of an elderly man sitting upright against the headboard, its glass eyes blankly watching the muted television on the cabinet in front of the bed. Linette is pushing 70, but the near-bald form in the bed must be over 80. Well, must have *been* over 80 when he'd croaked.

And did she say this corpse is her husband?

Ellis tries to do the math. Maybe this woman knows a loophole in the no-family policy that could reunite him with his wife.

His and Hers rolling suitcases stand next to each other near the bed. A man's watch and a bottle of cologne—props in an apparent charade—sit on top of one

106

of the bedside tables.

"Alfred, this young man helped me carry your ice from the machine. He looks just like you used to, back when you were on your feet. Strapping arms."

The corpses' shoulders, clad in striped blue pajamas, poke from the covers. Its head is mostly bald, but wispy white hairs coat the sides of its liver-spotted skull. The slack face looks like it might once have been owned by a kind man.

Linette lifts the bedcovers. "Come put those under here, would you?"

Ellis approaches the body and with each closing foot, the state of it further presents itself. The man's face and limbs have thickened with bloat and the skin of his head is multicolored; not with liver spots, but with the discoloration of decay. As quickly as he can, he lays the ice bags onto the corpse's chest, stomach, crotch, and thighs. He sees that the mattress cover is sheathed in plastic.

"Not on him! He's got trouble with his heart!" Linette snaps.

His heart isn't the trouble, Ellis thinks as he pulls the bags down to the sides of the dead man's body to surround and nestle him, trying to avert his eyes from the rot.

"There. Much better." Linette mock-scolds the body: "You're always leaving me too soon, aren't you?"

"I don't want to be rude," Ellis says, "but isn't he embalmed?"

"Of course! But I'm not some short-term, one-night-stand kinda gal! I stay at the motel for months whenever I visit, and I was here at the grand opening last year."

Ellis nods. "I see."

"All that work, would you like a drink?"

"No, I've already had too much, and I really should get..."

"I meant tea. You look like you could do with it."

"Oh," Ellis says. After his exhausting day, all the alcohol, and with the question coming from this woman who reminds him so fondly of his mother, tea sounds good. Maybe it will do the job of completely sobering him up. "Okay. Thank you."

"Take a seat," she says with that same familiar wave of her hand, and goes to the corner where the coffeemaker is.

Ellis chooses a chair as far from the body as possible. Linette makes him feel maudlin yet comforted. His own mother passed away three years ago; the big fucking C, discovered late when it was everywhere already. Before that, while Ellis was still a teen, she'd been widowed by the death of Ellis' father when he drunkenly crashed his car into a stop light. She dealt with this by pulling her son closer and holding him there for as long as she could. They'd gotten through their shared loss together, and Ellis always felt that, while growing up, he'd been loved as much as a boy could want; first by two parents, and then by one. Her eventual death hit him like nothing ever had before, and Emeley could barely help him at all. Maybe that bereavement was the start of their troubles.

"When did he die?" Ellis asks.

Linette totters towards him with a steaming mug. "A long time ago. Must be 12 years now."

Confused, Ellis stares at Alfred—still very much a body, though aspiring to be a puddle—as Linette takes a chair at the other side of the room with the bed now between them.

"Alfred died of a heart attack. Too much of that damn pipe, and too fatty a diet provided by yours truly, I imagine. Gotta take some blame for it, I s'pose, but he was the one who insisted on all those breakfast pancakes and bacon." Her eyes creep away from the body to Ellis. "He died in my arms, you know. I just woke up one morning, and he'd gone. I knew immediately."

Still baffled, Ellis says, "I'm sorry."

"Have you ever been in love?"

He points to the ring on his finger.

She frowns. "Rings don't mean much."

"She was mine," he says, voice hardening.

"You said 'was'. Past tense. What happened?"

Ellis doesn't reply.

"It's okay honey, you don't need to tell me. But if you decide to, you can take comfort knowing that I usually only talk to Alfred here."

The dead tell no tales, he thinks, and sips his tea. Earl Grey, sugared, with a splash of milk.

"Well if you've been in love, you'll know how hard it can be sometimes, won't you?"

He nods.

Sitting across from him in the gloom of the dim lighting, Linette's frail silhouette doesn't look much like the sturdy frame of his mother, but the voice...the words...

"Do you have children?" she asks.

The words sting. "No. It didn't work out."

"Same with us," Linette says. "Merl has already had so many Alfreds for me—four? five? This one looks quite a bit like my husband, but he must have lived longer than Alfred did. And Alfred's hair never lost its rich red color." She closes her eyes, remembering, then leans forward and strokes the corpse's leg through the blanket.

The truth dawns on Ellis. The body in the bed is a stand-in, a substitute for the real thing. "You must have really loved him."

"Love," she says, opening her eyes to look at the proxy form with longing. "Love, present tense."

Ellis knows what she means. Even now, after his and Emeley's disagreements; after their losses; after her death; after learning that she donated her body to Motel Styx; he still loves her. Love doesn't die, just because of a few problems. When it's real, like theirs, it lives on, even if it twists into a new shape. That's what Ellis tried to tell Emeley when she was alive, and that's what he's still trying to show her now.

Don't come looking for me, her note said.

But what the hell did she think he was going to do? He would never have stood for her being with another man in life, so why would he now in death? That level of protectiveness is natural, because love has a possessive heart.

True love is inherently selfish.

Ellis sits up with a new idea, one playing to the clear sympathy and emotion of the woman in front of him. "My wife died, and she left her body to this place." He tries to find a way to avoid insulting Linette: "I'm not... like the rest of the people here."

"Oh, darling—you don't think I already knew that?"

"Is it obvious?"

She adjusts her glasses and laughs a hearty laugh, one thick from smoking or booze. "It is to me, but I've got a knack for seeing the truth in people." She pauses a moment. "And now you've come to save your late wife from us degenerates, have you?"

"I can't stand the thought of someone else having her, using her like a plaything."

"Well, I understand a bit about possession. Pretty sure I'll be dead before I let Alfred go." She looks at Ellis straight. "*Don't* let Merl know you've got family here—that's a big no-no. He would have had to fight me off if this place existed and my true Alfred chose to come here after he died. I'd be a real Carl Tanzler type."

Ellis understands the reference from his necrotel research. The image of the notorious doctor and his brown-haired, papier-mâché corpse with the painted face—the body held together by wires, rags, and wax—flashes in his mind. It wouldn't be much worse than the rotting body in the bed before him. He pushes the grotesque thoughts away and returns to the task at hand.

"If I showed you a photo, can you tell me if you've seen Emeley?"

"I doubt it. I've only got eyes for Alfred, darling."

"Maybe you've heard someone say her name?"

"No one else speaks the names of the dead here. They've got numbers and they've got desirable attributes, nothing more."

"*I need to say goodbye to her.*" His voice sounded harsher than he'd intended. "She was vulnerable, and she'd never have come here if...ah, never mind. Maybe I should just give up."

"I think you're better than that," Linette says.

An eerie sense of déjà vu skips through Ellis' mind again; that was what his mother always said when he made the wrong decision: *You're better than that, Ellis. You're better than that.*

111

Linette's eyes twinkle, as though she knows exactly what she'd said. "Have you seen Merl's binders?" she asks.

The question comes out of left field. "Excuse me?"

"He showed them to me once, very proudly. Thick folders, heavier than one of these ice bags here, and he says they contain every body he's ever procured. I think it's a little tasteless myself—like keeping racy pictures of past lovers—but if you can get your hands on that and if she's really here to find, well, I daresay she'll be documented in those pages. He keeps them in the office."

A bulb clicks on in Ellis' fuzzy mind and he stands up. She's given him a lead. "Linette. *Thank you.*"

"Don't mention it," she says, smiling. "And don't be a stranger while you're here. Not much happens for Alfred and I these days, so a little gossip and a friendly face are always welcome. Us romantics need to stick together."

Ellis lays his empty mug on the counter and Linette rises to show him out.

"Stay safe out there," she adds, opening the door. "Don't you go aggravating anyone while you're poking around."

Ellis nods. "Good night."

When she closes the door on him, Ellis stands in the silent, meekly lit hall, letting himself feel hope for a few sweet moments. If he can get Merl to show him the binders, he'll know for sure if Emeley is already here, and if she is, *where*. He turns right and pads down the corridor to his own door but stops, hearing something.

Cant get my head strate

I liked the body I got but the place made me nervus. I dont want to hurt anyone, but Im not sure about the other custumers. Sum of them were real creeps.

Witness

From the far end of the corridor, in the direction of the wetrooms, comes a sound Ellis can only just make out: a low scraping. Then, just within hearing range, a whispered moan.

It's so late, but something prevents him from entering his room just yet.

In the distant dark, a hand reaches around the corner of the far wall and grips its edge.

"Hello?" Ellis calls, but keeps his voice low.

As he watches the hand, a ridiculous thought creeps into his mind: one of the many bodies of Motel Styx has dragged itself from its deathly state, freshly fucked and enraged by the way its tightening flesh has been abused.

You had me...now I get to have you...

The idea is so disconcerting as Ellis stands frozen

in the desolate corridor that he almost pisses his pants. However, something more than just a hand is emerging from the bend: a fuzz of hair, a pale forehead, and the unmistakable glint of an eye.

"Hello?" he says, louder, convinced that by raising his voice he can shake off the heebie-jeebies, or at least let the monster know it's been spotted.

The groan he'd heard rises, muffled but hoarse, wordless yet distressed, and the scraping comes again, fabric dragged across flooring.

Ellis is about to march towards the emerging shape to see more clearly when it suddenly vanishes from sight. There is a sharp *crack* and then a new figure appears. The lights brighten under its quick movements, flooding the section of hall and revealing to Ellis who it is: Yamamoto.

Feet apart, thick arms curled at his sides, the tattooed maniac stands nude before him, gazing at Ellis. His shadowed form is a patchwork of ink and blood and his shoulders heave with harsh breaths, like the hungry exhalations of a wild animal. Although Ellis can't see for certain, he believes that beneath the shadows Yamamoto is erect, thrilled by the draw of a new hunt.

A new prey.

The man strides forwards, and when the motion detector clicks into life and light pours over the naked man, Ellis sees something in Yamamoto's hand that flashes with each swing of his powerful arms.

Panic strikes Ellis. He digs in his pocket and fumbles for his keycard.

Yamamoto closes in, now just two rooms away, face bright with glee and red with blood, the thing in his hand sharp and metallic.

Ellis slams the keycard against the lock but nothing

happens. He swipes it again, heart racing.

Yamamoto laughs.

"Fuck!" Ellis hisses, realizing he's using Veronika's card, one that will never work. He pulls his own from his pocket and when the lock bleeps in approval he scrabbles with the handle, shoves the door inward and steps into the unlit room, slamming it behind him.

Somewhere through the oily blackness, Veronika stirs in bed but says nothing.

Ellis waits for a furious barrage of blows to hit the door: Yamamoto demanding to be let inside to sate his bloodlust.

All he hears is the bartender's sleepy breaths and Linette's muffled voice next door, drifting into the otherwise quiet space.

Ellis stands motionless, panting, listening for more movements outside.

Should he call Merl? Wake Veronika? *Leave immediately?*

No. That just won't do. He's come too far.

Maybe he was mistaken. Veronika's story of killers in the necrophile community was just campfire-talk designed to freak Ellis out, but maybe it worked. And had there really been a second figure out there in the corridor, or was the hand and face peeking around the corner just Yamamoto's, or one of his pulseless guests that the sick bastard puppeteered for his own amusement?

Ellis steps forward, jamming one of his hands on the gurney, stifling a cry as best he can. He finds Veronika's pants and slides her keycard back into the first pocket he finds.

Moving with tentative steps across the room, heart palpitating, Ellis lays down beside the bartender. He's wide awake, unsettled and disturbed, and thinking of how thin the line between life and death is, here at Motel Styx. Now though, with Linette's tip about Merl's binder, Emeley feels close enough to touch.

Whether Veronika, the deranged bitch once more snoring beside him, fulfills her part of their deal or not, Ellis will find his wife. Most grieving men would let it go and let her do with her body as she pleased, but Ellis isn't 'most men.'

Ellis isn't weak.

Ellis won't let Emeley have the last, petty word, no sir-ree.

Day Two

Motel Styx

"

The only things you regret are the things you never try.

"

- Dr. Mark Herbert (alias), Forensic Pathologist

Interlude:

Room 13 — The Honeymooners

The Roleplay Suite is cold, white-walled, and featureless, aside from the special cooling slab at its center and a panic cord by the door for emergencies.

"I can feel it startin' to worrrrk," Dana's naked newlywed husband Jabari says from the pillow.

Dana feels that uncertain tug in her chest that tells her, yes, this is scary, but yes, this is right, and yes, it may just satisfy her.

This brave new United States of America truly might be a better place for people like her, and the Lazarus Act might have come in at just the right time. Before she met her husband, she had been tempted to get a passport to travel to one of the world's other necrotels, in an attempt to secretly please the urges she hid from the rest of society. But like her many other plans—dig a grave? Get a job at a funeral home? Whisper it: *kill someone?*—she opted to drown those worrying feelings in streams of numbing vodka.

Jabari, who lies twitching on their motel bed, slurring his words and gradually becoming immobile, changed Dana's life. They'd met at Dana's first AA meeting and Jabari had been assigned as her sponsor. His well-deep eyes, baritone voice, and tales of a troubled upbringing gained her trust immediately. They both knew it was inadvisable for a sponsee to date a sponsor, but their connection was so strong that there was no resisting it. And when Jabari told her his life's motto, in that grandiose manner of his—*Be fearless, be true*—she opened up to him.

"I want the living, but...I can't stop thinking about the dead."

Dana had always been prone to anxious moods and paranoia, and the fantasy of sharing love with a departed partner who regarded her with total neutrality stirred her loins and soul. With an empty shell who could offer her the pleasures of the flesh without any chance of disdain or awkwardness, it wouldn't matter if she craved the abnormal, or disliked humanity, or masturbated to thoughts of making love to a road accident victim in a cold, cold mortuary. Without a pulse there would be no chance of ill intent or sneers from her companion, and while there would also be no chance of full sex, she always favored a stimulated clitoris to the sharp, breath-stealing jolt of penetration.

Jabari had shown no revulsion at her confession,

which unlocked a new intimacy between them. Within a year of meeting he proposed to her, and promised that he would offer her something truly special for their honeymoon.

While Dana would have preferred an actual encounter with a corpse, this fantasy scenario would do—for now.

Jabari's lips and tongue have started to fail him: "I'm fine, I'm fine," he breathes, repeating it like a mantra. Then: "Um fine. Uh fie. Uh hi..."

The motel's ridiculously named formula, SynthaMort, is clearly effective. She watches with a thrill as her husband's twitching limbs relax and the rise and fall of his bare chest reduces. The room's low temperature and the cooling board upon which Jabari lies do nothing to stop the exciting warmth Dana feels as she watches this pseudo-death consume her husband. He'd taken the motel's unique pill late the night before, rested alone for an hour in the motel's freezer-locker built specifically for this fantasy scenario, and then he was brought to this room by a motel employee while the tablet took effect. Now Jabari lies still and wordless, his pupils dilated to the extreme.

Dana's husband truly appears dead.

The motel's enthusiastic owner reassured them both that the effect of the drug would be convincing, and that if Dana becomes afraid she should check her husband's heartbeat. The Texan had shown her how, so she now squeezes her beloved's wrist and feels the sluggish, barely-there beat of his pulse.

Jabari is alive, but...not.

Dana had warned Jabari that, if he retains any awareness, she may act strangely while he isn't able to

121

respond. He replied, "Honey, you want to fuck a dead body. I doubt there's anything you could do that's more shocking to me than that."

Dana clambers up onto the frigid platform. When they rented the suite, the motel owner offered her some special, flattering lingerie that would provide thermal protection against the cold while allowing access to her most important areas. She had declined, and now wears only a thin, knee-length dress without underwear. She leans over Jabari and licks one unmoving eyeball.

No response.

She pushes the tip of her tongue into the other eye, lapping at his tear duct.

Still nothing.

She cups his balls; something that never fails to stiffen him.

Not the slightest reaction.

A second of fear clenches her heart, then lust takes over and she straddles his stomach, shivering at both the coolness of the room and the exquisite thoughts crowding her mind.

He's dead, she thinks. *I'm alone with my husband's cadaver.*

Gazing down at the blank, frozen contours of his face, she licks her fingers, reaches beneath her dress, and touches herself.

He's dead, and maybe he's REALLY *dead, and so what if he is? Because this is bliss, this is utter bliss...*

She nibbles Jabari's chilled earlobes then runs her tongue along the luscious crevasse of his lips. In no time at all she has cum for the first time and she cries out, her wail lonesome in the confines of the bare chamber. She tightens and clenches, too sensitive to keep rubbing, but that passes quickly when she clenches her teeth around her husband's noble jawline, then drags her incisors down to scratch past his throat towards the small nipples adorning the temple of his broad chest.

He's dead, and even if he's not truly dead, he will be one day, and perhaps I'll be the one to kill him...

It's a shocking thought but one she's considered before, and in the throes of her second orgasm she drifts into fantasy.

"I love you," she gasps at his prone form. "Rest in peace, because I will always love you."

She's overwhelmed as she clambers back up his body, pressing her inner thighs around his neck, her fingers dancing a frenzy against her clit.

He's dead, she thinks, welcoming the knowledge. *My husband is dead and I love him more than ever...*

Shuffling forwards, she smothers his motionless mouth with her vulva.

As she bucks closer to her third climax, she wonders whether she should ever let him breathe again.

Motel Styx

Bad Bedcovers, Bad Bodies, more like

Think my companion got mixed up with one for the wet rooms. He leaked everywhere, stank my room out, and stained the sheets. May I suggest keeping embalmed bodies totally separate, and using rubber bedsheets?

The Morning After

Ellis dreams of lying in a zipped body bag with Emeley as her body rots, surrounding him with the disconcerting warmth of squirming maggots and other byproducts of her putrefaction. Despite there being no light inside, he can see her face, the purples and greens of her papery, mottled flesh. He hadn't considered she might look like that, already going sour, but strangely it brings him comfort: regardless of her condition, in this dream she still belongs to him alone. There's no room for anyone else. No twin brother, no nameless perverted strangers. Just the two of them.

The dream ends as he relishes that first moment of warm but cold, moist but dry, perfect penetration.

When Ellis wakes, undisturbed, he first floats in that halfway netherworld between sleep and consciousness, where he often does his clearest thinking.

He loved Emeley; of that there is no doubt. He still does, but it's different now. Back then, right up until her last days, he still wanted to help her transcend herself. Now he wants to show her the extent of his love, the determination of it, and the power of his belief in her.

When they first met, she told him she was content to work at a pet store called *Whiskers*, serving up bird seeds, cleaning rodent cages, and boxing up live crickets for the reptiles. A till clerk earning less money than a decent waitress. Ellis had seen through the facade though: she only thought she was content because she was afraid of failure. Seeing her potential, Ellis had given her the strength and confidence to better herself.

As an accomplished personal trainer, Ellis encouraged her to go to the gym and drop a few pounds, and even personalized a workout program for her.

He told her she should study, read more, and socialize alongside him to help push her out of her shell.

He made sure she began applying for management roles instead of accepting her meager life at the animal store, and when that didn't work, he urged her to go into business on her own. Ellis managed to carve out a successful career as a personal trainer by standing on his own two feet, and with all her potential, so could she. She was better than that: he saw her as the owner of an online pet supply store.

But Emeley, true to form, squandered the opportunity. She pushed back, started arguments, and complained of the pressure. She whined about having to dip into her savings, even when Ellis explained that she'd need stock if she was going to sell it. And when she finally gave up, after barely a year of effort, a bitterness had risen between them.

After all he'd done for her, that change hurt, but his love was stronger than her lack of ambition, and it remains stronger than her petty decision to donate herself to a fucking body brothel.

She's better than that, even now.

In the motel bed, Veronika groans beside him. "Merl needs to invest in better mattresses. I'm stiff as a corpse."

Ellis looks down at his erection, deciding not to comment. His woozy hangover grows tense and he feels tired and stressed-out despite the sleep.

"Speaking of corpses, good morning to you!" the bartender chirps, but not to Ellis; to the cadaver still facedown on the Pummel Horse to her left. She reaches out and smacks its buttcheeks. The meat barely judders but Veronika moans with pleasure.

Ellis' erection softens and he climbs out of bed before she can cajole him into a quick morning session with the body. The thought disgusts him, but—with the way his head is—he can't be sure he'd say no.

He looks away as she fondles the lifeless gray form again. "Do you *have* to do that?"

"You weren't complaining last night. You were happy to watch."

"Fuck you."

"Oh dear. Someone got up on the wrong side of the bed this morning." She turns to him as he works the coffeemaker, her pixie cut spiked into hedgehog quills by the pillows. "You don't have to drink that crap, you know. I've got to do some accounting for the motel today, so I'll be in the back office if you want to stop by and drink something better."

The coffee machine burbles. A sour smell drifts up to his nose and Ellis thinks of the binder Linette told him about, and how it could reveal whether Emeley is already at the motel. He can trust a binder more than he can trust Veronika. He could hold proof in his hands. Ellis paints on a fake smile for the lying woman he'd fucked last night. "Actually, thanks. That'd be great."

"That's better," Veronika says, and stretches across the bed. "Last night was funnnn."

"From what I can remember, yeah," he says, partly because he needs to stay on her good side, and partly because it's true. His side-women have always been the mischievous, unstable sort, easy to send into a spiral with the wrong response, but good for sex. It's not enough to keep a feeling of betrayal from building though; he'd paid Veronika for a service that she isn't providing.

"You're no longer a corpse-virgin!" she exclaims.

Ellis recoils. "I didn't do anything to lose that virginity."

"Our secret," she says as she holds a finger to her lips. "You were there, so you played a part."

"I don't think so," he says, frustrated at how easily she riles him.

"Mind if I shower?"

"No, I don't."

Ellis watches her cross the room: nude, round of ass, tattooed, and horny for the dead. Bruises dot her throat and trail across her back. A ring of his teeth-marks darkens one of her thighs.

She stops halfway to the bathroom, dawdling beside the desk, and reaches for the envelope containing Emeley's suicide note that Ellis had leaned against the mirror. "Oooh, you've got mail..."

"Don't touch that," Ellis snaps.

She looks as though she's been chastised and offers

a playful *Oops, I've been naughty* face. Ellis' expression remains hard as she heads to the shower.

He ditches the coffee and returns to bed, remembering his drunken panic when he'd come back to the room the night before and Yamamoto had stormed towards him. As if those thoughts weren't enough to darken his morning, when he checks his phone he sees another message from Emeley's twin Damien:

The thing about running is you can be chased. I'll be touching down in El Paso mid-morning.

"Fuck."

Minutes later, Veronika steps out of the bathroom. "All yours," she chimes as she towels her hair dry.

Ellis showers while she redresses, and under the hot water he resigns himself to the imminent arrival of his brother-in-law, Damien. That fucking guy. By the time he's done, Veronika has already left to start her shift. With aggravation, he notices that Emeley's suicide note has dropped from the dresser onto the floor. He folds it in half and slips it into his pocket.

When he leaves the Greenlee Suite he follows the passage past a row of guest rooms, all blessedly silent at this early hour, and at the corner which turns towards the wetrooms, he inspects the wall where last night he'd seen the fingers and part of a face appear. The wall is smooth plaster with a varnished wood trim, and although there are a few scratches and some faded smudges, Ellis sees nothing to suggest the recent presence of a wounded guest. Considering the state that the wetrooms are no doubt left in, Merl's cleaning staff must be accustomed to clearing up blood and human remains.

Ellis stops at the Members Lounge and finds Merl making coffee behind the bar. At the far side of the room on a low stage, a woman dressed in a casual red pantsuit tickles the strings of an acoustic guitar. She sings about love into a microphone in a low, melodic tone, gazing into the eyes of a plastinated male corpse sitting beside her. It wears a shirt and red tie that matches the guitarist's outfit.

"Mr. Macintosh!" Merl bawls.

"What's this?" Ellis asks, gesturing toward the bizarre pair on stage.

"A traveling act I found online. She's trading performances for room and board and I've only got to feed one of them!" Merl chuckles. "So, she stayed the night, huh?"

For a moment Ellis thinks Merl knows about Veronika's visit to his room. Then, realizing what the man means, he offers his seediest attempt at a 'post-orgasm-with-a-post-life-partner' smile. "She was good, thanks Merl."

Merl lays a black coffee onto the bar for Ellis. "Just what I like to hear! Only the best for our VIP guests. Glad she met with your approval. I told you you wouldn't be disappointed!"

Ellis takes a bar stool. The coffee smells as sharp and unrefined as the stuff in his room. "One thing I'll say about the body, though. She wasn't quite to my...specifications. A little *too* perfect, if you catch my drift?"

"Well Ellis, we spoke about this."

"I don't mean the damage. I'm talking about her looks. In my application form, I asked for 'pretty, not beautiful.'"

Merl blinks. "Well sure, but why would a man want to settle for less than..."

"Because that's what I asked for."

Merl looks bewildered. "But *why?*"

Ellis improvises. "I find that kind of beauty a little false. Like porn, or an Instagram thot, you know? I like *real.*"

"Well, okay then," Merl says uncertainly, as though Ellis' request is stranger than any of the desires of a motel filled with necrophiles. "The customer is always right, I s'pose."

Ellis sips his coffee which, despite its crappy taste, soothes his hangover. "One other thing, Merl."

"Oh?"

"Yes, it's about..." Despite there only being the guitarist, her dead companion, and a couple of other patrons in the bar, he lowers his voice. "...Yamamoto."

Merl's face turns serious. "Okay. What?"

"Late last night he was in the corridor outside my room, and he rushed at me. Blood all over him, naked. I think he was holding a blade, too."

Merl is no Oscar-winning actor and his awkward smile fails to match his words. "Oh. Well. Yamamoto is an odd one, but he knows not to bother the other guests. I'm sure it was a misunderstanding."

"He came at me with a knife. I'm not sure how else that can be interpreted."

Merl sighs and leans over the bar. "Here's the thing, Mr. Macintosh. Some folks visit Motel Styx out of curiosity, or a kink, or an honest-to-God lifestyle choice, like myself. But then there are others like Yamamoto, who are...less easy to predict."

"Right," Ellis says, unconvinced.

"Now you saw Yamamoto yesterday in the wetroom, didn't you? The guy was in his element, an' when he gets

131

worked up that way, he can get a little overenthusiastic, shall we say. Wandering around dressed inappropriately, stuff like that. But don't you worry: he's harmless."

"Then why are you so scared of him? I saw the look on your face yesterday, when he came to his door. You looked nervous."

The Texan stretches his smile. "No, you're quite mistaken. Yamamoto is a valued guest at this establishment."

Merl might not understand people, but he sure understands how to keep his mouth shut. Ellis tries once more. "Motel Styx needs to build a reputation as a safe, friendly place for necs, right? I'm sure that the last thing you want is for a VIP guest to leave a bad review."

Merl's grimace is that of a man facing a messy chore; scouring a toilet or unblocking a drain. "I'll speak with him. Okay?"

"Thank you."

Ellis glances towards the stage again. The performer is between songs and staring longingly into her late lover's frozen eyes, one hand on the neck of her guitar, the other on the cadaver's preserved thigh.

A smell hits his nose.

"No!" Merl cries. "You know you can't bring Alfred into the bar when he's in that state!"

Linette is paused at the doorway with Alfred slumped in a wheelchair, his gray-green face leaning against his shoulder. A ripe stink billows through the bar. In the bright light of the morning, Linette still retains that maternal aura that reminds Ellis of his late mother, even when her face turns morose at Merl's outburst.

"I'll sort it," Ellis says, and goes to her. "Howdy, neighbor. How about we get Alfred back to your room, where he's more comfortable?"

"I just wanted a mimosa!" Linette grumbles.

"Merl can have it brought to your room, right Merl?"

Though cocktails aren't part of room service, Merl nods without hesitation.

Linette lays her hand on Ellis' arm, a mother's touch. He tingles.

She relents. "Okay. Fine."

As he accompanies her, pushing the wheelchair, Linette keeps her hand around his arm.

"I don't understand what the fuss is," she says. "It's not like he smells yet."

Ellis coughs out a chuckle. "Maybe not to *you*."

The old woman acts as though she didn't hear. "I like having a nice guest like you here, Ellis. You're a good man."

The words warm him, even if they don't quite ring true.

Motel Styx

"

In the UK, gambling companies are already offering odds on bets concerning which US celebrity will be the first to donate their corpse to a necrotel. I have it on good authority that [name removed] has already signed the contract.

99

- 'No Rest for the Dead', *USA Tonight*

Binders Full of Bodies

The back office door is propped open by a clear, acrylic gravestone bearing the same Motel Styx logo Ellis had seen printed on nearly everything in the gift shop. Standing outside, he hears groans that sound like Veronika's voice, and when he peers around the half-closed door he sees her seated at a chaotic desk with Chris standing behind her, massaging her shoulders.

"What the hell…" Ellis murmurs.

Chris looks up. "Well hello there, Mr. VIP," he says cheerily. "I don't believe your swanky—and apparently all-access—pass extends to these lowly staff quarters, so how 'bout you get the fuck outta here?"

"Woah there," Veronika says. "I invited him, Chris, so cool off."

Chris slides his hands down and brushes his palms over her breasts. "You were the one who said you were sore after you let this guy take a turn on you, but I thought you were looking for a *private* rubdown."

"Well I'm soothed now," she says.

"Fine." Chris leans down and pecks her lips with a *smack*. "I've got shit to do, anyway."

"Um. Chris," Ellis says, hating that Veronika is apparently hooking up with Chris, too, and hating the idea of asking him for help. "Before you go: you said you have access to the CCTV here?"

Chris puffs his chest. "Me and me alone, Mac. Why? You looking to revisit your witching hour wanderings?"

Veronika raises her eyebrows and cocks her head, intrigued.

"No. Something happened to me last night. With Yamamoto."

"Was that before or after you mistook the corpse-fridge for your room?"

"*What?*" Veronika asks, but both men ignore her.

"After. I saw him at the corner of the corridor, the one leading to the wetrooms." He levels his voice. "He charged at me holding a knife."

Veronika inhales, but something about the gasp sounds sarcastic. "My story in the lounge really frightened you that much? Now you're being chased by a murderous nec?"

"It wasn't just Yamamoto either. I'm sure I saw someone else there too," Ellis adds. "They looked weird. Maybe scared. Did he have any guests with him?"

"That's no one's business but Yamamoto's, Mac."

Chris smirks, looking at the bartender who winks playfully at him.

Ellis persists: "What if he hurt someone? Couldn't we just check the cameras?"

Chris shakes his head. "I can't show you shit. But I'll take a look myself and let you know."

Ellis watches the broad-chested man go to a door at the back corner of the office. The air between them seems tight until Chris shuts the door behind him.

"Some security guard. I don't feel safe at all," Ellis says.

"The best security guards are the ones who've worked for some bad people," she says, and wiggles her eyebrows. "Let's just say he knows how to handle himself, so we're all just fine. Maybe watch what you say around him though, huh?"

Ellis drops his voice. "He rubs me the wrong way."

Veronika—who is wearing a nametag that reads *Melody* today—eyes him with amusement. "And he rubs me the *right* way. When did you go to the fridge? Were you cutting me out of the plan?

"It was the alcohol. I wanted to see my wife. Hey, are you two an item?"

"What if we are? Maybe you should've peed on me to mark your territory."

"You'd have loved that."

"I'm a pervert, but I'm not into humiliation or pain." She tugs her collar down to reveal an especially purple bruise. "Not *usually*, anyway."

"I was drunk. You pissed me off." Ellis sighs. "So you're 'Melody' today?"

Veronika nods. "Melody the receptionist."

"Well Melody the receptionist, I had a deal with

your friend Veronika, so why don't you help me look around the office until we find out where the hell my wife is?"

"Veronika can be pretty nasty," she says. "I'll make you that coffee first. You look like shit."

If Emeley had ever spoken to him like that, they'd have had harsh words, but Ellis bites his tongue. "I grabbed a cup at the bar, so no thanks."

Veronika runs a hand through her pixie cut and stands, heading to the corner beside a bookshelf stuffed with documents. There's a large poster pinned to the wall: a pastiche of the famous old image of the cat dangling from a tree branch with the words *Hang in there!* written above it. The words are the same, but instead of showing a kitty, this poster shows a grayed corpse with a noose tight around its bulging neck.

As Ellis takes in the office—the morbid but playful posters, the paper-scattered desk, the droning air-con vent—he opts for a different approach in his quest to see the binders Linette told him about. "It's pretty wild, how far you've come."

"Me? I'm only from Valentine. Haven't come far at all." Veronika pours herself a coffee. "Or do you mean as a woman?"

"No, I'm talking about necs. It was only a few years back that you were forced to repress yourselves twenty-four-seven. Now there are motels all across the world letting you do exactly as you want, and legally. And I'll bet they're all run from little back rooms, just like this one."

"Pretty wild," the bartender says disinterestedly, before sipping from her cup.

"All those men and women, signing over their holes

for necs to use as they please, once they're dead. How many bodies do you think have been through here, since it opened? Hundreds? Thousands?" He whistles.

The bartender cocks her head. "What are you getting at?"

"I want to see the binders with all the past bodies."

"How did you..."

"I need to know if she's here. I need *proof.*"

"You can't take my word that she isn't yet?"

"Veronika!"

"Okay." She smirks. "You sure a normy like you can handle it?"

"You've got everything you could ever want here. We've given you your dead. Can you please just give me mine?"

"Fine. Nice speech." She dips low and takes an oak-green binder from a bottom-row shelf. "They're in these folders, all of them. This is the history of the motel, told through its carcasses. Merl's treasure room. He likes reminiscing, flipping through these like they're a box of personal memories." She leers. "Underneath that friendly exterior, he really is a sick motherfucker."

Ellis takes the binder from her and feels its weight, steeling himself for what he's about to see. The first page bears a date from early the year before. Then, on the next page, there is a bold number "1" followed by a pair of photos, which Ellis assumes are *Before* and *After* shots of the same nude woman with long blonde bangs.

On the left, she lies in repose: eyes closed beatifically, lips pursed. From the camera's position above her, Ellis can see the contrast between the paleness of her face and body, and the edge of the bruise-like darkness near her back where the blood came to rest after her heart stopped beating. She appears peaceful, with one thigh resting coyly over the other and hiding most of her pubic area.

The second image makes Ellis' stomach flip and the sour coffee from the bar climb his throat.

On the right, there's the same woman, but she's only recognizable by her hair. Her legs gape wide to show a mass of purple flesh, inflated by rot. Her eyes are cloudy eggs stretched open as if in distress, while a viscous black fluid has leaked from her mouth to stain her chin and neck. It's her skin that threatens to summon the full contents of Ellis' stomach, though, with its nauseating rainbow of reds, greens, and purples. Parts appear to have slipped from the bones, and despite there being no blood there are areas of the body that have been torn open, revealing glistening lower layers. A large section across her right shoulder has rucked up like carpet and her stomach has burst. Worst of all, her breasts are almost devoid of skin and have been reduced to shriveled sacs of slate-gray mush.

"That was Merl's first ever legally procured body," the bartender says. "Back then, he bought bodies from anyone willing to sign theirs over. Seeing as he was just starting up, he'd cut out any middle-men and pick them up before they were embalmed. That's why the first half of this binder is filled with ones that ended up like her: just, totally putrid. These days, the only un-embalmed bodies are the ones for the wetrooms, or those bought at a higher price for someone who wants to screw a ripe one, like the guy we call the Sniffer. It's a health hazard, so we generally burn them up before they get anywhere near this bad."

Veronika grins and squeals as Ellis flicks through the

pages. The photos are made up of at least three-quarters women, aged from late teens to the elderly, and all with the same repellent *Before* and *After* shots.

Used.

Sexualized.

Rancid.

"Why are there so many younger women?" he asks.

"Terminal cases with heart problems or cancer, suicides who want their families to benefit from their deaths. All sorts of reasons. And, *most* necrophiles are men."

"Can I see the latest binder?"

Veronika is about to answer when the door to the CCTV room opens. She snatches the binder out of Ellis' grip and lays it on the desk.

Chris barrels in and says, "It was a spoon."

"What are you talking about?" Veronika asks.

In a voice choked with laughter, Chris says, "Yamamoto. Last night. He was carrying a spoon while he walked down the corridor."

"What?" Ellis splutters. "It didn't look like a spoon."

"Well it was. A dessert spoon. Probably wanted to borrow some sugar! And sure, the guy was naked, but that's just the mark of a true eccentric, don't you think?"

Ellis frowns. "What about the other person I saw? The one who looked around the corner?"

"You must have been spooked: it was just Yamamoto. You really did have too much to drink. Double vision."

Ellis looks from Chris to Veronika and back again, appalled by the amusement creasing their faces.

"It's okay," Veronika says, and strokes his arm. "It's easy to get the creeps here, if you aren't used to it."

"It wasn't that," Ellis says, pulling away from her.

Chris takes a seat and places his hands behind his head. "Don't worry about it, Mac." He winks. "Happens to a lot o' corpse-virgins who visit the motel."

Ellis looks at the bartender in disbelief, but she just shrugs.

She'd told Chris he'd never slept with a dead body, that he didn't sleep with one last night.

She might have blown his cover.

"Go fuck yourselves," Ellis spits, and hurries from the room.

Decent!

The food at Café Charon was pretty good. Felt weird ordering the steak. Had to double check it was from a cow. Then the wife reminded me that it's cannibals that eat people, not necrophiles...at least not like that. ;)

Damien

Across the road from Motel Styx, Café Charon provides less tackiness and drama than its parent company. The menu carries traditional American fare, and following in that diner style, red stools and booths fill the interior. Framed images of tasty-looking cooked food hang on the walls. If it wasn't for the recently purchased gift shop t-shirts worn by the bachelor party in the corner—*It ain't cheatin' if her heart's not beatin'*, and, *Gashes to ashes, thrust to dust*—it could be mistaken for any regular restaurant.

Among the other patrons, Ellis is surprised to recognize one of the Christian protesters he'd almost plowed through the day before: a man in his fifties with a white prophet's beard and icy blue eyes. He looks less formidable now, tucking into a slice of key lime pie with a streak of fresh whipped cream smeared over his mustache.

Ellis is close to finishing his enormous plate of eggs, bacon, and biscuits with gravy—fuck the personal training diet—when a bell tinkles and his brother-in-law Damien walks in. It's like seeing a ghost.

The sight whips Ellis back to his bathroom at home. The door is splintered behind him, his shoulder is screaming from the blow, and in the bath Emeley lies motionless, staring not at him but at the ceiling. For a second he'd assumed she was deep in thought, the way she sometimes got when she looked lost in a trance. But no. The empty pill bottle and the stillness of the cooled water betrayed the true reason for her vacancy.

Damien's smug face usually makes Ellis want to kick his teeth in, but as the man crosses the floor Ellis feels a trace of relief at a familiar presence. Emeley's twin looks grave and gaunt, as though he's lost 10 or 15 pounds in the ten days since her death. He's wearing a fitted shirt and decent slacks, but without his business suit or one of his carefully curated outfits, he appears lost.

A cursory smile appears and vanishes from Damien's unshaven face and he sits down opposite Ellis without greeting him. Grief seems to have stolen the man's few likable qualities, polite respect being one of them.

"What are you doing here, Ellis?" Damien asks, slouching against the booth bench.

Ellis almost laughs. "Hello to you too. I could ask you the same."

Damien seems unimpressed.

The friendly waitress, a woman in her thirties with an overbite, neat round spectacles, and a chocolate-brown bun, strides over with a cheek-breaking smile. Her name tag reads 'Camila'.

"Welcome to Café Charon. Can I start you off with

some coffee?"

Damien looks her way and Ellis recognizes the telltale signs of his distaste: mouth creased at the edges, nostrils flaring. "Thanks," he says, his tone dismissive. He returns his stare to Ellis.

Camila leaves and Ellis decides not to break the silence. Instead, he glances out through the tall windows across the dusty desert road towards Motel Styx. The enormous skeleton looks ridiculous beside the motel sign; a kitsch and playful guardian over a world where the dead are refused their rest. In the parking lot, two familiar men—one bulbous and wearing a Stetson, the other well-built and dignified—stand beside a white Tesla. Merl is talking animatedly to Yamamoto, who instead of wearing his birthday outfit now sports a blue business suit. Ellis squints, not liking the stiffness of Yamamoto's body language. What happens if Merl is explaining to Yamamoto how Ellis had complained about him?

"I looked up the prices for this place," Damien says. "You can't afford them."

Ellis lays down his knife and fork, hiding his irritation. "You don't know what I can afford."

Damien snorts. "That brownstone you insisted on buying must have a helluva mortgage. And don't tell me you've managed to sell off Emeley's stock at last—she told me how much of her savings she burned through paying for that junk. Besides, you're going to need representation."

"For what?"

"I've spoken to my lawyer, he thinks we could sue you for wrongful death."

"You're throwing *that* in my face?" Ellis asks. "She left me...she chose to die."

"No, you pushed her to it."

"I didn't want this!"

"But I'm certain you want me to believe she went without writing a note explaining why. I know my sister, Ellis. If she did something desperate, she'd at least give us the reason. So where is it?"

Ellis glances around at the other patrons. "Can we keep this civil?"

"Oh *now* you want civility? Now that you've no longer got Emeley to..."

"There's no note," Ellis snaps. "If that's what you came all this way for, you wasted a trip."

"Then why are *you* here?" Damien asks, crossing his arms.

Ellis replicates the pose, tensing his biceps to thicken them. Keeping his voice low, he asks, "Are *you* okay with what they'll do to her here?"

Damien's face twists in disgust. "Of course not. It was just as huge a shock for me to learn she'd signed her body off to this place as it must have been for you. The only difference is that *you* were informed, while *I* had to go digging, making phone calls, speaking to nurses, doctors, then finally the medical examiner, who told me that the next of kin had already been notified of Emeley's contract with Motel Styx *more than a week ago.* Why didn't you tell me?"

Ellis gazes back at his brother-in-law, into the face that so closely resembles his late wife.

Damien's pale lips suddenly twitch and his eyes grow watery, a wretched sob hovering at the boundary— then the man's face tightens with anger. "You should have fucking told me."

"It's between Emeley and I."

"She was my *fucking sister*, Ellis. I need to know what happened. Why. What led her to do it."

"She was never happy," Ellis lied. "She had problems. Her business failed."

"And whose fault was *that*?"

"What's the point in mulling over it all right now? First things first: I want her out of here."

Damien's brow twitches. "You...you don't respect Emeley's right to choose for herself?"

Ellis laughs. "Are you kidding?"

Camila arrives with Damien's coffee. "There you are. Can I get you any..."

"No," Damien says.

Camila manages to retain her friendly smile despite Damien's sharpness, and retreats to the counter.

"So what's your grand plan then?" Damien asks in a whisper. "Are you going to get heavy-handed with the management? Or maybe you're going to spend the last of your cash bribing someone for her back?"

"You shouldn't have come," Ellis says. "You weren't there for her when she was alive, so why are you here now?"

Damien winces. "That's rich. I know how often you two fell out, because she got in touch with me whenever things got tough."

"Didn't reply too often though, did you?"

"*She was my sister*," Damien says again. "That doesn't just disappear because life gets in the way."

"You hurt her. She said that your job meant more to you than she did."

"*I* hurt her?" Damien shuts his eyes for a couple of seconds, and when he opens them the sorrow has broken through again. "She changed after she met you."

"That's what people do when they fall in love," Ellis says. "They realize what matters. They evolve."

"She distanced herself from the family."

"She didn't need you anymore."

Damien sighs. "You don't know anything, Ellis."

Ellis sips his coffee, despising the encounter. "Go home."

Damien's eyes shimmer. "I just...wish she'd reached out to me sooner. Properly, in person, and not just in text messages. Maybe if she'd received more support from us after she lost the baby, she would..."

"Don't talk about that," Ellis says. "Not now. Not ever."

Damien wipes his eyes. "Look. I doubt I'll ever understand why she donated her body to this place, and I hate it, but Ellis, whatever you're planning...it's madness. Why don't you just explain to the owner who you are, and..."

"They can't know who I am!" Ellis hisses. "Or who you are. We're family of the deceased, and that's not allowed." He leans across the table. "Think of Emeley when I tell you this: they don't just molest the bodies. They dress them up. They degrade them. They cut them into pieces and *then* molest them. Is that what you want? Does that sound like something I'd let them do to her? Do *not* fuck this up for me!"

Ellis jumps when the bell above the door rings again.

Wearing his tailored azure-blue suit and crimson tie, Yamamoto looks like a grave-faced movie star standing on a red carpet: slicked-back hair immaculate, eyebrows sculpted, and stubble groomed with military precision. Yamamoto clearly has the kind of money that would make Damien's corporate managerial income look like chump change, and Ellis look like a bum. His expression is blank when he meets Ellis' eyes, but menace hangs above him like a stormcloud.

Ellis lowers his gaze to his coffee, remembering how Yamamoto's muscles rippled as he prepared to drill into a dead woman's forehead. Ellis had felt relief at the idea of Merl speaking to Yamamoto about his behavior, but now, caffeine-fueled and with a full stomach, Ellis realizes the danger he has put himself in: he'd snitched on the most dangerous man on the property.

Damien twists his neck around and calls for the waitress. As he does, he glances towards the door, sees Yamamoto, and wilts.

"I'll be with you in a moment," Camila says. She shows Yamamoto to a table on the far side of the café beside a window looking out across the bare, sand-blown desert.

Damien watches, entranced, fully aware that locals and tourists don't dress like this man. "He's one of them, isn't he?"

"Yeah. The worst of them."

Despite their differences, Ellis wants to tell his brother-in-law how Yamamoto rushed him the night before. No matter what Chris claimed, Ellis is sure that Yamamoto had been wielding a knife. It would be a relief to open up to a non-necrophile about the horrors he'd witnessed at Motel Styx, but now isn't the time—not with Yamamoto just meters away from them, not with Emeley still lost somewhere within the walls. Ellis is about to invite Damien to come for a stroll when a shape appears beside them.

"I heard you," says the bearded protester he'd seen at the counter. The man's frost-blue eyes are wide and unblinking, his loose white shirt near-ecclesiastical. "You're staying here, aren't you, but you understand how wicked this place is."

Ellis is torn between maintaining his deceit as an experienced necrophile, and agreeing wholeheartedly with what the guy said. However, Emeley is the mission and a preaching churchie won't make him stray from her. "This is a private conversation. Please leave us alone."

The four bachelor party members filter by behind the bearded man, and as they leave Café Charon, the wild-eyed Christian remains at Ellis' and Damien's table, one of only five remaining people within the establishment. Ellis sees that even now, the whipped cream from the man's key-lime pie remains stuck to the hair above his lip.

"Paying respect to the dead is one of the traits that makes us human," he says, eyes fierce and focused. "And what takes place here is an aberration. They don't just keep the dead from their rest, they desecrate their bodies, like prostitutes fit for defilement. It is rape! It denies our very humanity!"

"Sir, please..." Damien begins.

"I heard you both. You aren't a part of this abomination, so will you not stand with me? Stand with my brothers and sisters in Christ to help us fight this monstrosity?"

"Look pal, you need to leave," Ellis says.

"They don't just abuse the dead, oh no—they *create them*. They slaughter the innocent and hand their bodies over to the sinful for their base pleasures. Since we have stood outside together in the name of Christ, pleading with the motel guests to see godliness, our numbers have waned. Our loudest—our mightiest—have been snatched, slain, corrupted! It is an…"

The bearded man's eyes bulge from his skull. Air bursts from his lips.

Camila drops the half-full coffee pot and shrieks so high that her voice breaks in unison with the glass carafe shattering on the floor.

Ellis looks up and time stops for a moment.

Standing behind the man, Yamamoto stares meaningfully at Ellis, then whips his arm to the side.

"

These people are freaks! What are they going to pimp out next? Animals? The world's going to shit in a rocket-powered hearse.

"

- Jeff Radnor Podcast

Bloodbath

Something warm speckles Ellis' cheek.

Yamamoto shoves the bearded man forwards, bending him over their table. His head scoots aside the plastic ketchup bottle along with the small metal basket holding the single-serving jam packets, and his arm crashes into Damien's coffee mug, erupting its scalding contents over the window and the bench seat next to Ellis.

"Jesus Christ!" Damien yells.

There's a ruby flash of sunlight in Yamamoto's hand: a thin chef's knife streaked with blood. Ellis rises from the bench, bracing himself for impact, but Yamamoto's eyes are on the back of the protester's white shirt and the scored line of red his blade released. As Ellis backs away he sees the damage the knife has carved: a deep ditch

153

through fabric and flesh, oozing the slimy yellow of exposed fat.

Damien sits aghast.

Like a carpenter striking a nail, Yamamoto rams his weapon into the protester's spine.

"Move, Damien!" Ellis bellows, backstepping towards the diner's kitchen hatch, planning to circle the tables to the door.

With a scrape of metal against bone, Yamamoto wrenches the protruding handle downwards. The protester howls and Yamamoto licks his lips, his face suddenly dripping with the man's blood.

Damien jolts out of his daze and hauls himself from the booth.

"A big mouth," Yamamoto says as he pulls his victim up from the table.

The man makes a gargled cry and blood waterfalls over his beard, tainting the remaining whipped cream a pinkish hue and splashing across Ellis' abandoned plate. Yamamoto turns the protester around and shoves him back onto the grisly table.

Ellis breaks for the door. The waitress is nowhere to be seen as he hurries a lap around Café Charon, keeping his eyes on Yamamoto to ensure the lunatic stays distracted. Absorbed and frenzied, the killer brings the knife handle down against his victim's front teeth, breaking them with a crunch.

"Run!" Ellis yells to Damien.

The protester's arms flop and hang limply over the table edge, hands level with his scrawny thighs. Barely alive, his lips flap over shattered incisors. Yamamoto's expression turns lascivious, eyes rolling as they had when Ellis watched him loom above the two female corpses.

Damien reaches Ellis just as he throws open the door and the desert heat rolls over them. Camila emerges from beneath an empty table to join them, tugging a key from her apron pocket. She locks the doors to Café Charon, but not before Ellis sees a new abomination taking place inside.

Yamamoto has the Christian on his knees and is holding him upright by the hair. The lunatic has unzipped his pants, extracted his erection, and directed its head between the protester's gory lips, apparently unconcerned by the jagged fence of broken teeth.

Damien stares slack-jawed through the glass.

The scene in the café is worse than anything Ellis has already witnessed at Motel Styx. It wasn't a spoon he'd seen Yamamoto holding the night before, and it wasn't solely Yamamoto in the hallway. It was a knife, and it was murder. *This* is murder, and the ghost stories of Yamamoto's homicidal streak are fact.

"I'll get Me-merl," Camila says, her voice shaking. "I'll ge-get Merl."

"How far are the closest cops?" Damien asks. "This is fucked."

As fucked as it is, Ellis doesn't want the cops to come because they'll shut the place down, ask for his ID, and the distance between him and Emeley will grow once more.

"I'll get Merl," Camila repeats. "I'll get Merl." Muttering the same words, she scuttles across the road in a dawdling zig-zag.

"He's using...his mouth," Damien says, his tone dreamlike as he watches Yamamoto. "That man is dead..." he says, pointing. "...and he's using his mouth."

"Stop looking," Ellis says, thinking he might vomit.

But Damien is so transfixed that Ellis can't resist turning back to the door for one final glance.

The bloodied protester seems dead. As Yamamoto slips his length in and out of the responseless mouth, he jabs the knife through the corpse's eyes in time with each thrust.

Right.

Left.

Right.

Left.

Ellis remembers Yamamoto storming towards him down the corridor the night before.

That could have been me, he realizes. *That could have been me!*

He has the strangest thought: if he had been killed, at least he would now be in the same position as Emeley. And as he watches the madman have his way with his freshly murdered victim, something shines star-bright in Ellis' mind: he really will stop at nothing to make Emeley his again. He won't allow her to spend her final days before she is cremated in this hellish place. He will have his rightful goodbye.

Ellis tears his gaze away from Yamamoto when he hears gravelly footsteps behind him. Merl looks furious and Chris looks grimly resolute as they march side-by-side towards them from the motel.

"You two!" Merl calls. "Let's clear some space, shall we?"

"That's the owner," Ellis says.

"I know," Damien says, then raises his voice: "Are the police on their way?"

Merl holds up his hands. "Let's take a deep breath now, shall we?"

"What the hell kind of place do you run here?"

"Sir..." Merl starts.

"Don't *sir* me. Answer me!" He jerks a thumb back towards the café. "I've seen your interviews—how dare you act like this is an innocent place where consent takes priority, if psychos like *that* are free to harm living people?"

Smirking, Chris says, "I don't see anyone living in there, Mister."

Damien's eyes are pits of fury. "*Do you think this is funny?!*"

"Of course not, but what's done is done," Chris replies. "It's unfortunate, but what goes on in Motel Styx, stays in Motel Styx. It's an internal matter."

"Chris," Merl says, his voice a hushed warning.

The Head of Security shuts up but his sneer remains in place.

"I can't apologize enough," Merl says. "I assure you, we are going to do everything we can to ensure it never happens again."

"*It's still happening!*" Damien screams, pointing at the monstrosity inside.

Merl tugs a black clicker from his pocket and presses a button. "That man's suffering is over."

Café Charon's metal shutters descend with a clatter.

Damien looks astonished. "What are you doing?" he asks, as Yamamoto and the mutilated man vanish from view.

"Denying him the audience he wants." Merl adjusts his Stetson. "Now, forgive me, but I don't believe we've been introduced. If you don't mind me asking, how are you acquainted with my friend Mr. Macintosh here?"

Ellis has the urge to answer for his brother-in-law,

but that would raise suspicion.

"We're...friends," Damien says, growing unsteady on his feet.

Ellis releases a breath.

"We met online," Damien continues. "He told me he was going to visit your motel, so I said I'd meet him here for some food to discuss how he's finding it."

"Care to show some ID?" Merl asks.

Damien scoffs. "Considering what I've just seen, do you think I want *you* to know who *I* am?"

Merl holds up his hands again. "Well now I suppose that's fair." He sighs. "Okay then, cards on the table: we've all seen something like this before, haven't we? As necs, it isn't exactly uncommon for someone in our ranks to go rogue. Doesn't make it any less a tragedy and Yamamoto will get exactly what he deserves, you can trust me on that. But please consider how hard it's been to make Motel Styx a viable business, catering for people as slandered as us. I can tell by the car you drive and the shirt you're wearing that you're a professional yourself, sir, so I'm sure you understand why I want this situation to be tackled with...decorum?"

Damien laughs, but a glance at Ellis straightens his face. Perhaps he'd recalled Ellis' words: *They can't know who I am...or who you are.*

"A man just died," Damien says, but the certainty is fading from his voice.

"I know. He did *not* deserve that and we will conduct a thorough investigation."

"But still, the police..."

"They'll be called in time, when we have all our ducks in a row. Now, as you were an unwilling witness to this disaster at our sister property, I am open to discussing compensation..." Merl leaves the sentence hanging for a moment, then wafts his collar. "Perhaps you'll come to the lounge, have some water, and discuss this in more comfortable surroundings?"

Ellis is sure that his brother-in-law is going to refuse the bribe and maybe even expose him, but Damien's expression becomes one of weariness rather than refusal. "Okay. Water sounds good," he says, sounding drained. "Thank you."

"Mr. Macintosh?" Merl asks.

Chris looks at Ellis curiously.

Ellis eyes Merl. "I thought you said Yamamoto was harmless."

After a pregnant pause, Merl asks, "Are you okay?"

Ellis realizes that Merl's look is asking a different question: *Can I trust you?*

"I'll be fine, Merl. I just need a moment."

Chris keeps watching him, calculating, until Merl says, "Come on," and they lead Damien across the road to Motel Styx. "I'll be in the lounge later, Mr. Macintosh. As will you. Drinks on me."

For a moment Ellis bristles with unease, but as they leave him standing alone in the sweltering Texas heat, he recognizes the opportunity in front of him. They can busy themselves with damage control and he can get back to the task at hand.

Motel Styx

If you feel like you're being watched…

You are. Cameras all over the place, kinda defeating the privacy that was promised.

Camera Feeds

It's become obvious to Ellis that he can't rely on Veronika, so as usual he has to depend on himself instead.

Following the café 'incident'—and Ellis considers the cold distance of the term—Merl has a lot of cleaning up to do. He'll need to convince Damien to stay quiet, to clear up the protester's body, and to somehow get Yamamoto to leave the premises. Things are moving quickly and Motel Styx's staff will be thin on the ground, giving Ellis the chance to recommence his search for his wife.

The office is clear, just as Ellis hoped. He closes the door behind him and glances at his watch: the second body from his VIP package is due to be delivered to his room sometime in the next half-hour and an unanswered door will be suspicious, so he'll have to hurry.

Ellis grabs the latest binder from the shelf and crouches behind the office desk. Keeping his head low, he lays the binder on the floor and flips through the pages, bracing his stomach against the grotesque images: a dismembered woman whose jaw has been flayed skinless; a man's decomposed face, sprayed with liberal gluts of gray-white fluid; an elderly body of indefinable gender with a realistic flesh-colored dildo jammed into its gullet. Ellis doesn't see any reason for the tasteless *After* photos and fears what he might see if Emeley has already been here.

The page dates crawl closer to the present day, charting the soiled corpses that have passed through Motel Styx's doors, into its bedrooms, then into its incinerator.

He finds a photo of "Alfred", Linette's most recent one anyway, and he's surprised how fresh it was when it first arrived two months ago. She must have it out of the fridge more often than not.

Despite there being a number of bodies at the end of the binder with *Before* shots but no *After* shots yet, clearly still in use or maybe still in transit, Emeley isn't among them.

With a growl, he shoves the binder back into its place and rises to his feet. He wants to be happy she isn't here, but how long will he have to extend his stay to get her back? He's about to storm from the room when the door in the far corner catches his eye: the one Chris vanished through to check last night's CCTV.

Ellis realizes that he's probably being filmed right now, but hopefully Chris won't check the previous feeds any time soon. Once Ellis finds Emeley, even if he manages to get off the premises before he's discovered, things will likely turn *really* sour. That's why he should prepare some leverage: evidence against these fuckers, which he may one day use to close the place down for good.

The corner door opens to reveal a cramped, darkened space the size of a walk-in closet. There's a monitor on standby, a computer, a chair, plus protein bar wrappers and an empty sports drink bottle littering the desk. The back wall is pasted with photos of fitness models, but someone—Ellis assumes Chris—has drawn bloody wounds and bruises over the images with a ball-point pen.

Ellis shifts the mouse and the screen monitor sparks to life, revealing eight streaming CCTV feeds. They're crawling with activity, and one in particular draws his attention: Merl in Café Charon, gesturing and holding court with Yamamoto, who has finished with the protester and now stands calmly beside the corpse, glazed in its blood. Merl irritably plucks a post-coital cigarette from Yamamoto's mouth. The CCTV system is simple to use, so Ellis cycles back through the café footage to find the moment Yamamoto slashed the Christian protester's back. Using his smartphone, he films the murder and its aftermath, including Merl talking with Yamamoto instead of calling the cops.

There. Leverage.

Curiosity grips Ellis. Perhaps he has time to learn what's *actually* been happening at Motel Styx, under its thin veneer of respectability.

He checks through the different feeds and finds one recording the wetroom corridor. He begins to scan back through the footage to earlier that morning.

At 3.12am, a skinny, nude figure leaves a door at the end of the hall; the wetroom in which Ellis saw Yamamoto drilling through women's bodies just yesterday.

The man that emerges is not Yamamoto. This wire-thin, jerky form has a mass of curly hair that bounces as he limps down the hall towards the camera. He's strewn with blood and each step seems to bring him pain. In

163

the murky amber light he drags a lame foot behind him, the ankle of which is twisted, and when he reaches the corner nearest to the camera, Ellis sees that black tape is stretched across his ruddy cheeks and mouth. The man pauses, glances back, then places a weak hand around the edge of the wall for support.

Ellis' mind numbs as he changes camera and sees himself standing drunkenly outside Linette's door, watching this poor man's fingers curl around the plaster. With a sinking feeling he returns to the other feed and watches the owner of those fingers, the scrawny, injured guy, clearly in need of help and peeking fearfully around the wall.

That morning, rather than helping, Ellis had frozen with terror.

Yamamoto exits his wetroom and marches towards the waif, one arm raised and clutching something long and thin. Once he's caught up, Yamamoto wrenches the bleeding man by the shoulder and slams the handle of the tool against his head. The waif's legs buckle.

When Yamamoto turns the corner, *bingo*, Ellis sees the truth. The madman is clutching a knife—not a spoon, as Chris claimed—*a fucking knife*. The *same* fucking knife he'd used to murder the Christian in Café Charon, in fact. Ellis watches in dulled shock as Yamamoto chases him to his room, then returns to drag the unconscious man by the arms back through the wetroom door.

Chris, the Head of Security, had lied to Ellis to cover up for Yamamoto.

Why?

Ellis has seen so much horror already that even the shock and terror he'd felt in Café Charon only lasted as long as he'd been in Yamamoto's immediate vicinity, but with a freight-train-crash of understanding he recognizes how terrified he is.

It isn't just the guests of Motel Styx he needs to be wary of; it's Chris too. And what about Merl? Veronika? Arnie? *Linette?* Fuck, even the girl in the gift shop is probably hiding something.

He listens to the silence of the office beyond the door and decides to check one last detail on the CCTV. Something about the waif-man's face and body language felt familiar.

On a hunch, Ellis finds a camera feed recording from above the Members Lounge entrance. He skips back through the hours to the night before while he and Veronika were drinking together after her shift, then winds the feed back to the early evening when he'd still been sober, arriving after he'd received the first body into his room. He pauses the screen.

Veronika served a young man wearing a baseball cap with spots across his forehead and chin. His skinny frame is unmistakable: it's the same man Ellis saw escaping Yamamoto's room, then being beaten about the head and dragged back inside. As grim as this discovery is, the hat unnerves Ellis even more.

Ellis shuffles through more camera feeds until he finds one recording the corridor that leads from the vestibule behind reception to the fridge. In the live stream and happening right now, Arnie is rolling a gurney down the passage. Ellis checks his watch; that must be his second body. He's run out of time.

Just one more minute...

Growing frantic, he rewinds the feed back to the early morning hours. He sees his onscreen self standing at the refrigerator doorway, raising Veronika's stolen keycard to the lock, and then looking guiltily up as Chris interrupted him.

When Chris appears on camera, the view of the CCTV feed is looking down over his shoulders. He's carrying a pile of clothes, at the top of which there rests a baseball cap; the same cap Ellis saw the waif-man wearing in the bar, just hours before he was hauled unconscious and bleeding back to Yamamoto's wetroom. And while the man was likely being tortured there, Chris had been taking his clothes in the direction of the crematory.

Chris knew.

That's nec-on-nec violence covered up and enabled by the security outfit.

The door behind Ellis suddenly opens.

"Fuck!" he barks.

In the doorway, Veronika props a hand on her hip. She wears a knowing smirk. "You may just *have to fuck*, if you wanna get yourself out of this."

"Chris lied," Ellis blurts. "Yamamoto killed someone last night. And now he's killed someone at the café. We're all in danger."

The amusement drains from her face and for the first time she seems defensive. "No way. Though it might not seem like it, Yamamoto follows a strict code. You don't have to be afraid of him."

"Does he seem like a man in control? He murdered *two people*, Veronika!"

She drops her mouth open, feigning astonishment. "Is that the reaction you want? You need to get your ass out of the office. Aren't you due your second body?"

Ellis can't comprehend how she can be so calm. "You're fucked up."

"You know what they say about people in glass

houses, Ellis. And if you aren't in your room in half an hour when I knock, I'll tell the whole damn motel about you."

Motel Styx

"

Out-of-date phrases like 'corpse desecration' no longer make sense, now that we have the concept of consent. The people who claim that we're violating one of the most significant steps in our evolution don't understand the very concept they're leaning on. Evolution itself evolves.

"

**- Senator Marian Rossi, appearing
on *America Uncut***

The Second Body

Arnie is waiting at the door of the Greenlee Suite when Ellis returns, and at Ellis' invitation he rolls in the gurney bearing a sheeted body. With the previous gurney and the corpse-draped Pummel Horse still inside, the only way for Ellis to distance himself from all the death in the room is to sit on the bed.

Ellis glares at Arnie, feeling his tolerance for the motel's residents and staff scurry away from him. "Do you ever feel guilty about the things you do to the bodies, Arnie?"

The lanky embalmer looks astonished. "What?

Why?"

"Just wondering."

Arnie wipes a hunk of greasy hair from his forehead, as if to clear space for his thoughts. "I, uh, guess so. Sometimes."

"When?"

Arnie screws his face up into a parody of concentration. "Like when you saw me yesterday and I was supposed to be prepping one but I was, uh...not. Then I feel bad."

Ellis knows he should stop, but can't. "Is that the only reason, though? Because you didn't have permission? Not because you're *fucking a corpse*?"

Arnie holds his gaze, then exhales and hangs his head. "I know it's...not good. I'll stop if I ever meet someone who's, uh, not dead. But I can't yet." He looks up. "What about you?"

Ellis absorbs Arnie's sloped shoulders, unclean hair, and creased brow, and has the impression of a profoundly lonesome man. His anger subsides into sickened pity, as Emeley drifts back into his mind. "I guess it's no worse than the things we do to each other."

Arnie nods and lifts the first body off the Pummel Horse, laying the dead woman back down on her gurney to push her out the door. One wheel squeaks a mournful exit theme.

Unable to stop himself, Ellis suggests, "Why don't you start by resisting the bodies you aren't supposed to touch?"

Arnie doesn't turn or acknowledge Ellis' words. "I'll have someone come collect the apparatus, unless you want to keep it? You know, for this one?"

"I asked you a question. Why don't you resist the

urge?"

As Arnie reopens the door, his face becomes indignant. "Your second body is right there, sir. Why don't *you?*"

Ellis bites his tongue as Arnie closes the door behind him.

He doesn't know how long he sits, staring at the new sheeted body, looking for the courage to stand up and reveal it. *Cowardice isn't in your blood, boy*, his mother always told him when he was small and scared. Ellis can hear it like it was yesterday, the accusatory and humiliating call to action. He sucks in a deep breath and tugs the cover away from the woman's face and for a second thinks it's Emeley. The hair is dark enough and shorter than that of the first cadaver, the breasts similarly petite to his wife's. The face is more serene than Emeley's ever was, but he supposes that death will do that to you. While the jawline is narrower and the brow larger, the similarity to his late wife taunts him.

"Well," Ellis says. "Are you happy now?"

He watches the corpse's thin lips, envisioning Emeley's own fluttering in a way that used to both comfort and irritate him. He remembers how she spoke: the twitch of her neck as the sentences left her mouth, the musical timbre of her words.

"You'd laugh if you could see me now," he says. "You'd cover your face with your hands and make those awful squeaking giggles until I told you to stop."

He almost hears her faint answer.

"That's not fair, is it?" he replies, reaching out and taking her chin in his fingers.

He pictures the body's glass eyes coming to life and flicking his way. His grip on the cool jaw tightens.

"You don't get to do this to me," he says. "It's not fair. All I ever did was love you. Any...mistakes I made, were as much your fault as mine. You know it's true."

This time he sees Emeley bite her lips together, as she did whenever she wanted to speak her mind. He presses his hand across the lower half of the corpse's face and shoves it hard into the gurney.

There's another knock at the door.

Ellis re-covers the body and hesitates a moment before letting Veronika inside. She has changed into a pair of crimson Converse and a rockabilly-style red dress decorated with skulls and black roses.

"Ooh, body number 2!" she says, almost skipping to the gurney near the bed.

"Leave her be," Ellis says, still half-seeing his wife lying there.

Veronika stops, arms stiffening at her sides. "You should be careful how you speak to me, mister. Who knows what I might do."

"Don't threaten me," Ellis says. "Not even playfully."

"Chris is right to be suspicious of you, we both know that, so you can't be mad."

"It has nothing to do with Chris. You said you'd help me and you aren't. I have every right to be fucking pissed."

Her lips curl in amusement. "You aren't the first husband to come searching for his late lady-friend. Can't bear the thought of someone else touching her, can you?"

"We've been through this."

"I've seen your member file. How you describe the rental companion you're looking for. It's Emeley, isn't it? Not too pretty, only slightly above average? That's what you think of your wife."

"What I think of my wife isn't your business."

"If you don't think she's anything special, why are you so goddamn averse to letting the rest of us take a turn?"

Ellis slaps her.

Veronika cries out, clutching her reddening cheek. Then she punches him across the jaw.

Ellis stumbles back, shocked. "Ow! You *bitch*," he says, lifting a hand to his face.

"This is your last warning," she says. "You try to order me around, or hit me again when I haven't given you permission, then I go straight to Merl."

Ellis rubs his jaw. "If you aren't going to help me, I'm not going to pay you, so why haven't you gone to him already? What are you getting out of this?"

She smiles, looking wily despite the handprint he'd left on her cheek. "There's not much to do out here in the middle of nowhere. Gotta take my fun wherever I can find it."

He frowns. It would be so much easier if this cunt just played ball. "I can pay you double to take this seriously."

"No, Ellis, I don't think you can." Veronika pinches a small section of the sheet in her hand. "Have you taken a look at her yet?"

"I said leave her be."

Veronika gasps and drops the sheet. "Is it *her*?"

"No, it's not Emeley."

"You're sure? Did you have a grope?" She whips the sheet off the body and drops it at her feet. "Oooh! Merl really *does* save the good ones for the VIPs."

"Are you going to help me?" he asks, hating how weak he sounds, how *manipulated*.

The bartender takes the second body's head in her hands. "Can we help him?" she asks. Then, moving the slack mouth open-and-closed, she says in a high voice, "*I think he should help us first...if he's man enough.*"

Ellis stares. "Do you disrespect all the guests like this?"

"Only the assholes. Doesn't feel great, does it?" She smiles unpleasantly. "Look, if Emeley signed a contract with Motel Styx, then I can find her personal file for you. That'll tell you everything." She moves the corpse's mouth again. "*You just gotta give us some sugar, sugar.*"

"I'm not in the mood for this crap." But she's baited her hook well. "How can you be so casual, after everything that's been going on?"

"It doesn't matter what's happening at Motel Styx as long as you leave here with your wife, right?" She pulls her dress up over her head.

To Ellis' disgust, his lower half refuses to stay angry.

She's right though: deep down, it doesn't matter, not really, as long as Emeley is there at the end of it.

What had Chris said?

What goes on in Motel Styx, stays in Motel Styx...

She points at the gorgeous, lifeless form on the gurney. "Look at her. Just how I bet you like them: obedient and quiet."

Ellis suddenly advances on Veronika, feeling vengeful yet turned on.

She squeals with delight and strips off her clothes. "Get her on the bed!"

He clouds his mind as he lifts the dead woman off the gurney, smelling chemicals and the bitterness of her insides mixed with the clean fragrance of cedarwood. With one arm under the shoulders and the other the thighs, he lowers the cadaver onto the bed. As he lays the head gently onto the pillow, Veronika reaches around him from behind and massages the crotch of his pants.

"Touch her," she commands.

Ellis despises that he's hardening in her hand. The naked shape before him still feels familiar; a stand-in for the true object of his desires.

"This is what you want?" he asks the body, disdain in his words.

It lies there pale and limp, mouth ajar.

"Yes!" Veronika says, and slides the fingers of one hand beneath his waistband.

Ellis pinches one of the corpse's flat, pink nipples and takes a guilty thrill in its lack of response. It has no will, other than to please him.

Just like it should be...

"She's so slim," Veronika says, as she strokes his cock with one hand and unzips him with the other.

"Yes," he replies.

He wipes the dark hair over the stiff's face to encourage the illusion, turning the empty vessel into a captive rich with erotic potential. It revolts him; it arouses him. He won't fuck it though.

He will *not* fuck it.

Veronika peels his pants and underwear down to his thighs, releasing his rigid cock, and then clambers onto the body. A yin-yang of life and death, she spreads her thighs over the corpse's face. With its features hidden by her flesh but a few wisps of dark hair still visible beneath the bartender's rear, it's easier for Ellis to alter its identity to suit his needs. On all fours, the bartender lowers her face so that her chin hovers just above the body's tightly curled pubic hairs, then opens her mouth and extends her tongue to him invitingly.

Ellis turns back to the desk mirror. Behind his reflection, on the bed, the corpse is smothered and Veronika has her jaws open; a pair of sex dolls.

You're better than this, he thinks.

But he yanks off his pants and shirt, circles the bed, and grabs the living woman by a scrunch of short hair. "You see that?" he asks, pointing at the glass. "Look at yourself."

She doesn't resist him.

"*Look at yourself!* You love it, don't you?"

Keeping a handful of hair wrapped up in his fist, Ellis climbs onto the bed with his knees between the corpse's legs. He pulls Veronika towards his hard length and her mouth gapes as she envelops him. The movement forces her to add more weight to the body, which causes a flapping gust of air. Ellis isn't even sure which hole the noise came from.

Veronika giggles around his cock, then tugs her head back. "They do that sometimes," she says, undeterred.

A funky smell rises from the corpse as Ellis eases himself back between the bartender's lips, then thrusts. She gags and he relishes the power he's regained over her, watching her bare ass squirm as she grinds on their motionless guest's face. He pushes until he feels the back of her throat press against the head of his erection, enjoying the sight of her eyes watering and the urgent writhe of her hips. He imagines the cadaver suffocating on her crotch, as though it needs air to breathe; imagines it's Emeley lying there, shoving her face into Veronika's pungent pink flesh.

After a while Veronika's movements become frantic and she cries out, dragging her head backwards again.

Close to ejaculation, he slips from her mouth.

"Cum into her!" she begs, and with her thighs still engulfing the corpse's skull she uses her fingers to pry open its cold pussy.

Ellis stares at the almost-tempting cavern of flesh spread before him.

"Push it inside!" she says. "Go on!"

It's Emeley...Emeley's body...your body...

"No!" he yells, and rams Veronika's gasping face into the corpse's clean, dead cunt.

With the pickled tang of formaldehyde in his nostrils, Ellis sprays the bartender's hair and the pale thighs of the cadaver with cum.

She looks up at him, grimacing, and lifts her fingers to a glob of semen that covers her parting. "Ugh! I just washed my hair this morning!"

"Oops," Ellis says halfheartedly, savoring her aggravation. "There's fresh towels in the bathroom."

"Asshole," she says, climbing down off the bed and sauntering off to shower again.

Ellis lays down on the bed, spent, relieved. He'd still resisted, but the pull of this goddamn place horrifies him. It burrows into you.

A while later, the bartender returns from the bathroom redressed, her hair stringy from a fresh shampoo. "Meet me in the theater across the hall in fifteen minutes," she says as she's leaving. "I'll bring Emeley's file, not that you fucking deserve it."

"Why the theater?"

"You'll see."

"Hey, do you know where my friend Damien is?"

She shrugs and bangs the door shut.

Ellis grabs his phone to check for any messages from

his brother-in-law, but the screen is empty of notifications. He tries to call, but the phone only rings endlessly. He types out a short message.

Hey man did you leave?

The text sends and Ellis stares at the chat, expecting a near immediate reply. The typing dots begin to dance at the bottom of the screen. They disappear, then reappear, then leave again.

Ye

Though the reply, with the 'yes' missing its 's', is strange coming from a man who usually texts in full sentences, Ellis doesn't have time to solve a new mystery. Instead, he considers taking the gun from his luggage as protection against the freaks and villains of Motel Styx, but decides against it when, no matter what he does, it's too prominent to conceal.

He leaves the Greenlee Suite wondering if Veronika is actually about to give him a lead, or if her promise is going to send him down yet another dead end.

Michelle von Eschen and Jonathan Butcher

Expected more for the cost

*Rooms were what a poor man would think feels expensive
and the entertainment was lacking. Thought it would be
an oasis, but it was a mirage.*

Interlude:
Room 12 — The Performer

Ruth stands in the middle of a small, unfurnished room, and lowers her clothes to the floor. She stretches her limbs, bends and twists to open up and limber her body for her performance. Raised a dancer, the importance of a pre-show ritual doesn't escape her and, just like the act, every move of the preparation is planned, choreographed down to the minutiae.

She reminisces as she readies.

Her upbringing was liberal and supportive, and her household was comfortable with nudity. Her parents plus both older siblings sunbathed naked during summer, left the bathroom door open while bathing or showering, wandered the house without clothes, and held full conversations with each other wearing only their birthday suits. There was no taboo concerning the pale peach of Ruth's mother's flesh, the roasted coffee of her father's, or the mellow gold of hers or her siblings'. Their skin was simply who they were, and genitals were treated as being no more embarrassing than noses or ears; why should they hide one part but flaunt another?

Ruth was informed of the pleasures her body could offer if she, or someone she trusted, touched her in the right ways. But when puberty hit she found herself disinterested in the bodies of her fellow students and those of the polished celebrities cavorting on social media and in movies. They held no mystery.

Then she met Scott.

Ruth thinks of him and smiles as she smacks a bottle of lotion against her right palm, relishing the feeling of the cream dropping to the lid before she spreads the oily substance over her body, adding extra to her most delicate areas. She likes to remember Scott as she prepares for a performance, regressing to the moment she encountered what felt like the first truly *uncovered* form she ever knew.

It was during a Biology class in middle school when their round, dainty teacher Mrs. Cranwell first rolled Scott into the room. The class sat wide-eyed, some giggling, some pointing, some nervous, all enraptured. Scott was an anatomically correct skeleton suspended by a hook onto a metal frame on wheels, and the moment Ruth saw him she knew that something important was happening to her brain.

She sat up straight.

She touched her hair.

She felt...warmer.

So that's what we look like, she remembers thinking,

now 20 years later in a necrotel, admiring the sheen of her oiled skin. *That's how we really look.*

Scott was a replica, but young Ruth had been no less intrigued by him than if he'd been real. While she'd seen skeletons in movies and cartoons, she'd never encountered a full-scale representation in person. He was magnificent: the hollow caves of his eyes; the panache of his lipless smile; the delicate points of his fingers; the brawn of his ribcage. He hung prostrate before the class, silent and unashamed, but Ruth found herself in an exquisite purgatory, pulled between the urge to look away for modesty's sake, and the desire to drink in every detail of his brazen form.

That night in bed she touched herself and imagined she'd had the courage to rise from her seat and caress Scott before the class and her teacher.

Now she runs through the movements she will soon enact, here in Motel Styx's special theater, with as much attention to how they will impact her own pleasure as to the enjoyment they will bring to those watching.

After a deep inhale to center herself, she pulls on a thick and hooded black robe and moves to stand in front of the body that encapsulates all she has ever been drawn to. Stripped of clothes, skin, muscle, tendons, and organs, it is only bones now, and while the partners the motel provides for her to perform with are always nameless, for Ruth, each one is precious and unique.

The light above her turns from red to green, indicating that beyond the single-sided glass she can't see beyond, her audience has arrived.

She will not disappoint them.

Motel Styx

"

I wish I could go for the entertainment without having to screw a corpse. That's just too rich for me.

"

**- Delilah Short, Opinion
Piece in *Crystal Thinks***

The Contract

Feeling as though the filth of Motel Styx is sinking into his pores, Ellis finds the theater door just down the hall from his room and opens it onto a small space lit by dimmed, red-bulbed sconces.

At first glance the room resembles a chapel, with rows of pews facing the far end. No pulpit or altar sit centered in that space however, only thick red velvet curtains pulled closed. A red neon cross—albeit an up-side-down one—glows on another wall.

Veronika sits on one of the pews closest to the curtains. She turns around and offers a coy smile, the expression suggestive.

Ellis would like to wipe that look *right* off her face.

She raises a finger to her lips and whispers, "Ruth

isn't here too often, so I couldn't miss the show. Thought you might enjoy it too."

Though Ellis is tired of her distractions, he can't help but remember the woman from the lounge, book in hand, unassuming. What did Veronika call her? "Ruthless?"

Veronika nods and pats the seat next to her. "The Bone Fucker."

Ellis takes the center aisle and he can see that the pews have been padded with more of the same red velvet as the curtains. He sits beside Veronika and wonders what she is going to show him now, what new low he is about to reach.

She presses a button on a keypad built into the armrest at the end of the pew and the curtains open to reveal a large frosted white square on the wall that turns transparent. It's a window and what Ellis sees through it makes him stand and cover his mouth to stop himself crying out.

On the other side of the glass, that same woman from the lounge—wearing only a long, open-fronted cloak—kneels atop an altar that may once have adorned a real church. Lined with blue velvet and swirled carvings, the item's beauty contrasts with the abomination taking place on its surface. The woman has draped her cloak back over her far shoulder and is caressing her nakedness against a disconnected but correctly-arranged skeleton. Her latté-toned skin contrasts with the osseous yellow-white of its parts.

"She's an exhibitionist, like Yamamoto," Veronika says, seeming to keep her voice hushed more out of reverence than necessity. "Only, she likes them dry and long-dead. She rubs herself against them like that, or fucks herself with the bones." Veronika hits a different switch that allows the sounds of the Bone Fucker's pleasure to leak into the theater. "Merl got the idea from the six-feet-under clubs, where couples fuck in coffins while a camera shows them gettin' it on. It's a one-way mirror. She can't see us, but she knows we're watching. It's quiet here now because it's daytime, but some nights she gets a full audience."

Ruth, the Bone Fucker, has positioned herself above one femur and is rubbing her clit against it with such aggression she seems to want to sand the bone smooth. Ellis remains standing transfixed as she kisses the ribcage, her black nipples trailing against the lower pelvis. There's an art to the act, a dancer's grace to the way she moves the bones like pieces of a disjointed marionette; a dismembered figure animated by its lover's desires. Her moans intensify and she builds a sweat, droplets hitting the dry bones beneath her squirming body.

For a moment Ellis forgets why he's there. "Holy shit."

"The holiest," Veronika replies solemnly. "Some worship gods; she worships death and makes love to it."

Ellis sits back down as the woman lays on her front flat against the dilapidated form, then dips her long tongue into the mouth of its skull.

Veronika slaps something knowingly onto his lap, whacking the erection he didn't realize he had. He wakes from his trance and looks down to see a gray file.

"I printed Emeley's contract off for you. I don't know if you're looking for closure or something else, but you'll likely find it in there. Some answers, and maybe more questions."

Ellis looks at her and can't hide his gratitude. She

actually came through for him. "Thank you. Seriously."

"It's straightforward. The file has her contract and a few photos too, but I thought those might be a bit difficult for you to look at, so I made sure they were beneath the other papers."

Ellis thinks. "Why wasn't she in the binder?"

Veronika shrugs. "I don't know the method to Merl's madness."

Unconvinced, he rises again and walks to the light of one of the sconces, opens the folder and finds the contract. It was signed electronically so he finds nothing as haunting as more of his late wife's handwriting, but holding the document still feels intimate. According to the date, she'd filled it in the day before she died, a last-minute decision, and below her personal details Ellis sees information that almost makes him retch: what she was willing to let the guests of Motel Styx do with her remains.

Oral penetration: check.

Vaginal penetration: check.

And—*Jesus fucking Christ*—anal penetration: check.

Ellis grinds his teeth. She'd never let him fuck her ass.

Costumes: check.

Theme rooms: check.

Emeley wouldn't roleplay as the slut or the virgin for Ellis, but she'd ticked her identity away for strangers.

The contract feels to Ellis like a catalog of personal insults.

Dismemberment/wetroom use: no check.

At least she'll still be whole and there's little chance he will have to go through Yamamoto to find her.

Another paper in the file has a table with two columns, one labeled *DATE* and the other *ISSUED TO.* In the date column, five dates over the course of the last week are written.

"What's this?" he asks and holds the paper out for Veronika to examine.

She takes the sheet and Ellis thinks he catches a spark of knowing on her face, but it's gone as quickly as it appeared. She glances at him but can't meet his eyes. "Um...it's like a library card in a book, back before computers. Only instead of when the body is due back to the fridge, it's all the dates it gets 'checked out' and where it was taken to."

"She arrived before me? She's been here all this time?"

Veronika shrugs again.

Ellis feels a repellent tide rise up inside him as he realizes what this means, what it *really means*. "Each one of these is a timestamp for when somebody fucked my wife."

"Yes—unless it was Linette and she just bored Emeley's head off."

Her lighthearted tone summons a snarl from him. He stomps towards her, grabs her by the arms, and lifts her from her seat.

"Don't..."

"You've known this entire time!"

"I didn't know how to tell you."

"Bullshit!" he barks, and slams her against the wall beside the glass. "You've been fucking with me since the moment I got here."

Veronika makes a panicked glance towards the performer, who has straddled her fleshless partner's hips as though it is penetrating her. The Bone Fucker pays them no mind.

"It's one-way glass, isn't it?" Ellis says, emboldened. "She can't see, so I could..."

Veronika knees him in the balls.

He grunts, releases her, and staggers backwards. "You poisonous fucking cunt!"

"Lower your voice."

Her tone is so sharp that he shuts his mouth, clutching his testicles with one hand. "I could get you fired, you know."

Veronika laughs, clearly shaken but catching her breath. "Who's the one making the threats now?"

Ellis raises the checkout sheet and stabs a finger at the column labeled *ISSUED TO*. "Who's in Room 21? That's the only place she's been."

"I can't tell you about the other guests. Discretion is top priority. But I'll meet you after my shift and take you to the refrigerator..."

He shakes his head. "I won't wait that long. Does someone have her right now?"

"She wasn't checked out when I printed this."

"Then take me to the fridge."

She checks her watch. "I can't do that. I've gotta go. I'm running dinner service at Café Charon tonight." She pulls a name tag from her pocket and pins it to her shirt: *Camila*, like the real café waitress. "Merl has a hell of a cleaning lady, but he gave Camila some time off after the Yamamoto stuff."

Ellis judders from the reminder of the slaughter.

Despite their encounter, Veronika gives him a sympathetic smile that turns lascivious. "Look, I don't have time to take you to the fridge, but I've got a few minutes." She nods to the Bone Fucker, who is now smelling the skull of the skeleton while using a lubed rib on herself, living up to her name. "I could blow you while you watch the show."

Ellis stares in disbelief, his balls still throbbing from her attack. "You don't know when to stop, do you?"

Veronika sighs. "Fine. Drop by the bar later?"

"I don't plan on sticking around. I'm sick of this place."

She pouts. "Aww."

"And I'm fucking sick of *you*."

The playful expression melts from her face. "Well. I hope you find your wife, Ellis. I'm sure she didn't mean to hurt you by donating her body to us." She turns cold. "She just threw the bathwater out with the baby."

Her words steal Ellis' breath.

She can't know...

Before he can recover, Veronika paces to the door. "See you around," she says, and leaves without another look.

On the other side of the window the Bone Fucker whines, shuddering atop her skeletal lover, then presses a button on the wall beside her. The window turns opaque once more.

Motel Styx

"

People act like it's sick, but it's just plain sad. The customers of Motel Styx need help, not condemnation, and the popularity of necrophilia reflects the needs of an increasingly infantilized culture. No one can let go anymore, everyone's lost. Something is rotten—no pun intended.

"

- Teri Jensen, Podcaster for *You Heard it Here*

Decomposition Waits For No One

Ellis paces back to the Greenlee Suite to prepare, but before he taps his keycard he hears Linette wail in the next room.

He bangs on her door. "Everything okay, Linette?" he calls, half-fearing Yamamoto had selected his next nec to kill.

Moments later the door opens and Linette stands before him, still wearing her purple robe but with a dejected look on her face. "The ice only does so much. Alfred is going to muck again."

Facing Yamamoto would have been terrifying, but Ellis wasn't expecting to deal with a disintegrating corpse. He doesn't want to touch rotting flesh, or smell it, or even see it.

"Oh, I need to..."

"Come in for a moment, will you?" she asks, reaching out and taking him by the wrist.

He wants to tear his arm away and refuse, but since arriving at Motel Styx, Linette is the only person who has shown him any kindness without an obvious ulterior motive.

The air is murky as he follows her in; a waft of freon and moldy Italian meat, draped in a layer of flavored candle fragrance. Ellis coughs.

"I know, sorry," Linette says. "He's ripe. The air conditioning broke during the night and Alfred's been out of the fridge for too long." She looks distraught. "I shouldn't have asked you in, but I always find this part hard. You know: getting ready to say goodbye."

He nods because he *does* know. That's how he feels now, preparing to bid a final farewell to Emeley.

In Linette's bed, Alfred's face is a nightmare. He looks green in the low light and his skin has gone past bloating and begun to sag. His mulched eyelids are slits and Linette has piled paper towels beneath his chin to catch a dark viscous mess leaking from his nostrils and mouth.

Ellis hovers by the closed door, pitying Linette.

You're better than that, he hears his mom tell him.

"Would you like something to drink?" Linette asks. "Or some Vicks for your nose?"

"No," he says, stomach somersaulting. "It's okay."

"It doesn't get much easier," Linette says. "Sometimes I wonder if I should stop coming here, but...I'm not ready yet."

She looks so frail, standing there beside him: thin hands twisting and tumbling over her paunch, her lined face drawn with melancholy. Ellis reaches out and lays a hand on her shoulder. She moves into his embrace, no doubt starved of real affection.

"I'm sorry, Ellis. You must have enough on your mind, without me bothering you."

"It's fine," he says, feeling torn between a need to leave and an urge to salvage something good from this place.

"Any luck getting to Merl's binders?" she asks.

"Emeley's already here, and she's been...used."

"Oh. That's terrible."

"You should leave, Linette."

"I know, but..."

"It's not safe here."

"You mean that nasty business in the café? I never dine there anyway. I would rather take my room service here, with Alfred."

"Not just that. I think that bad things happen at Motel Styx more often than anyone realizes."

"Are you going to leave too, then?"

He loosens his hold on her. "Soon. But I know which room Emeley's in. I'm going to get her."

Linette looks him up and down, shaking her head. "Oh, Ellis," she says. "Perhaps you should take your own advice and get out while you can. You don't belong here."

He looks at her and sees his mother, her chest almost concave with weight loss, still up on her feet and attempting housework despite her terminal diagnosis.

Unlike the kindness on Linette's face, his mom's admirable life-long toughness turned bitter in the end. *You're too soft on her, Ellis Edward Mercer*, she'd said about Emeley. *That's your problem, and you know it.*

So after his mom passed, he'd toughened up.

Linette crosses her arms. "When Alfred died, the first time, I couldn't even view his body. I had my sister take care of the identification and we chose a closed casket funeral. Eventually that huge spike of pain subsided and I just missed him terribly. I needed to see him again, *my way*." She angles her head, inspecting him. "Surely you don't really want to see her here in Motel Styx? That shouldn't be your last memory of her."

She's wrong though. Ellis currently has three 'final' memories of his wife, and he despises them all.

The last time he saw her alive, they'd fought the night before, and when he said goodbye as he left for work her tears had already dragged the mascara from her eyes.

The last time he saw her dead, she was in the bath where he found her, frozen and unignorable, like an insult.

The last time he heard her words, he was reading her cruel suicide note.

Ellis wants a more fitting final memory.

You're too soft on her. You're better than that...

"I failed," he says at last, angry at himself, at Emeley, at Motel Styx.

"You think you failed your wife?" Linette asks.

Ellis doesn't correct her, and feels the anger he's been holding back flood through him, the tide finally coming in.

"I'm sure you didn't," she says, frowning. "Death is

never easy to face, but it's the only certainty we have. It weakens you, and you need time to adjust."

With those words, she ceases to remind him of his mother. His mom was too smart a woman to offer pithy observations, and too bold to suggest that he accept any kind of weakened state. She would have understood what he was doing here, why it mattered so much, and why he can't just let it go.

Now Linette just looks like a sad, lost old woman who can't tell shit from Champagne.

"Go home, Linette," he says, and points at the pile of human sludge in the bed. "Can't you just move on with your life like a normal fucking person? The real Alfred would be *disgusted* if he knew what you were doing."

Tears spring to Linette's eyes, but Ellis is done caring about anything beyond Emeley. If Linette thinks he ever did, she's wrong.

It's time to fix this mess.

Motel Styx

Worst man alive

There's no way my Eddie would have signed up for a program like this! The owner Merl took advantage of my dying husband! Motel Styx is a scam. Shut it down!

Harem of the Dead

Room 21 has a plain door like all the others. Ellis knocks.

Nothing.

He tries again, louder.

Still nothing.

He's about to hammer when something prods his back.

"You need to leave, Mac."

He turns around.

Chris has a stare that could melt a glacier. "I want you gone, just like your pal."

"Damien?" Ellis asks, caught off guard. "He left?"

"Yup. You'd be smart to do the same."

"Is he going to the police?"

"Merl gave him several thousand good reasons not to."

"He took the bribe?" Damien is money-oriented, and Ellis wouldn't be surprised if in the past he'd strayed into criminal territory—but could he really be paid to ignore murder?

Of course not. Something happened.

Chris nods. "Merl is keen that Motel Styx avoids any more bad press. His arguments can be pretty compelling."

"And what about..." Ellis is about to say *Yamamoto* when the man himself circles the nearby corner.

Yamamoto is dressed in fresh clothes, but above his crisp white collar his tanned neck is speckled wet with blood.

Ellis manages to avoid shrinking away, but his jaw drops with shock. Nobody speaks, but Yamamoto offers a polite bow of the head as he passes by.

"Now I know what you're going to say," Chris says. "But he'll be out of here by tonight. We're taking care of it."

Ellis bites his tongue. Once he leaves, he's going to report every single one of these fuckers to the cops.

He bangs the door of Room 21 again.

"What are you doing, Mac?" Chris asks.

"Knocking on a door."

"Got a friend in there, or something?"

"That's right," Ellis says. "You know him?"

"Can't give out that information to a guest." He steps closer and takes Ellis by the upper arm. "Why don't you just..."

Ellis shakes him off. "Don't touch me."

Chris smirks. "Or what?"

Unable to resist any longer, Ellis pushes his face close to Chris'. "Or I'll tell the cops everything about Yamamoto...and you."

The security guard flaps his lips: *pshaw.* "You don't

know shit, Mac."

"I know whose clothes you were carrying to the crematory last night."

Chris' mouth curls. "Beats me where you dream this shit up."

Though it's tempting to reveal the proof he has on his phone—the CCTV footage—he asks, "Where's Merl?"

"In his room. He has company."

"What number?"

"Right next door. Room 20."

Ellis brushes past and walks the short distance to Merl's room, riding a surge of adrenaline. When he knocks on Merl's door, he hears the Texan groan inside.

"What is it?" Merl yells. "This is my private time!"

"This can't wait!" Ellis yells back.

There are footsteps and the door is tugged open, wafting incense and the sounds of meditative bell-ringing into the hall.

Holding the door ajar, Merl wears a silk robe and his customary Stetson. His cheeks are red and slick with sweat, his mustache damp. "Mr. Macintosh, didn't see you at the bar earlier," he says, panting. "You caught me... uh...sampling my wares."

Ellis ignores a meaty, pungent odor beneath the incense. "I need to speak with you, urgently."

"Well, I guess you've seen wilder things today than what's going on in here." Merl beckons him. "So come on in."

Ellis enters the room and feels like he's stepped into another world. As Merl closes the door, Ellis sees that the walls and ceiling are cloaked with shimmering textiles that mutate the square space into something softer and almost circular in shape. There's a deep chill from the air con and an array of circulating fans which flap the silken material. The floor is a field of pillows surrounding a low bed in the center of the room, upon which are piled naked bodies defined by a mixture of sexes, body types, and ethnicities; a veritable harem of the dead. They lie in tangled disarray, some facedown, some on their backs. It takes Ellis a long stare to recognize that this heap of flesh contains six separate cadavers.

Merl goes to the bed and lies down on the uneven surface of skin, keeping his robe closed as he drapes himself with a color-wheel of pliable limbs. "This better be good, Mr. Macintosh."

"I don't know where to begin," Ellis says.

"Mind if I carry on? I need to be out of here again in an hour." Merl reaches to the floor for a squeezy bottle of lube and, turning over, begins to grease a muscular ass.

"Did you bribe Damien to stay quiet about what we saw Yamamoto do in Café Charon?"

"Sure, o' course I did. Chris took care of it." Merl uses his other hand to wet a rounder, plumper butt he could use as a pillow. "I meant what I said: that man's death was a tragedy, but he was at a necrotel, so what did he expect?"

"Probably not to be skullfucked over breakfast!"

"Blunt, but fair," Merl says, shaking his head with regret as he pumps his hands in unison. "We tend to attract all sorts, but I decided right from the start that I'd *never* judge another soul for their tastes."

"Since bribes are business as usual here, what will it cost me to find out who your neighbor is, the one in Room 21?"

"What?" Merl asks. "That was a curve-ball. Why?"

Because I want to find my wife and go, you sick fuck.

"Because," Ellis says, suddenly struck with unexpected emotion. A tremor enters his voice. "Because..."

Merl opens his robe and displays a stubby, purple prick. He looks up. "You're not...crying are you?"

Ellis snorts and wipes his sleeve across his eyes. Adrenaline crash. "It's been quite a day."

"Well, it's a bit awkward, you gettin' all weepy while I got my dick out. And I can't give out confidential info about our guests."

Ellis' vision is blurry as he gazes at Merl, naked and surrounded by the dead. He's wasting time. He needs to take the final, necessary steps, and get out of this godforsaken place.

"I won't keep you any longer," he says. "I may have to check out early, Merl."

"Oh now, don't be like that—you've still got another body to enjoy," Merl says. He rises to his feet, hands smothered in sex-grease. "How about you go back to your room, an' I'll get Arnie to bring you somethin' special, eh? Give you a nice treat after a tough day. Then, if you like, I'll give you the same cash as I gave your friend and we can go our separate ways. Okay?"

Ellis leaves the sordid room, his head buzzing with visions of blood and death.

Motel Styx

"

It's a disgrace, is what it is. What happened to red-blooded men craving a beautiful living, breathing hardbody? Makes my trade more difficult too...Me? Well sure, I'd do a three-way scene with a stiff. How much you offering?

"

- Harry Steel, porn performer for *suckfuckchuck.com*

Head Games

Back in his room, Ellis waits for the familiar knock of Arnie's bony knuckles.

He's broken every pencil from the box of 36, except one, which he raises to his eyeline to read the engraving on its side: *Emeley's Pet Supplies*. No creativity to the name. No drive to make the company work. No wonder it failed, and no wonder she lost most of her savings buying all that stock, which sits unsold and pointless in a rental garage Ellis is still paying for.

Alongside all their disagreements and those messy final weeks (which he *won't* think about right now), money troubles contributed an extra layer of stress, struggle, and strife. Ellis felt that he placed his wife on the highest pedestal, yet she'd managed to ruin everything before spitting one final time in his face and giving her remains to Motel Styx.

Snap.

He drops the pieces into the trash, sensing a symbolism but unsure what to make of it. Then he collects the silenced gun from his luggage and slots it into a holster hanging at the back of his waist, hidden beneath a baggy red sweater. Red for blood. Red for vengeance.

And now he waits.

The wooden rapping comes and Ellis moves for the door. Given Merl's promise of Arnie bringing "something special" for him, he expects to see another sheet-covered gurney. Instead, the lanky fellow holds a stainless steel cloche in one hand and a towel over his arm behind it, like a waiter at a fancy hotel. He's even combed his greasy hair to one side.

"Hi, Arnie," Ellis says. "You don't ever sleep, do you, bud?"

"I take power naps," Arnie says, seeming taken aback by Ellis' friendly greeting. "I've got you a gift from Merl."

"What a treat," Ellis says. "Maybe you can put it on the desk."

Arnie steps inside.

Ellis closes the door. "I meant to ask you something, actually. I saw you with a gurney the other day, and the sheet slipped a bit," he lies. "Gorgeous little thing underneath. Dark brown hair. Little titties. Had a white scar just above her eyebrow."

Arnie lays the lidded platter down in front of the mirror, frowning.

"I was wondering how I might get my hands on a body like that? She was just my type. Do you know who I mean?"

Arnie shakes his head. "No I don't think so."

"I think you do, Arnie," Ellis says, standing in front of the shut door. "I think you know exactly who I mean."

"Sorry, I really don't."

"Don't lie to me."

"I have to go," Arnie says, heading towards him.

Ellis isn't a fan of confrontation—not with men anyway—but Arnie is skinny and nervous, and pent-up anger has been building inside Ellis since he arrived. "Did you fuck her, Arnie?"

Arnie shakes his head again, harder, loosening his stringy hair into a mop once more. "No, I didn't."

"You think I don't know what someone like you would do to a piece of ass like Emeley?"

Arnie's eyes widen. "You *knew* one of the bodies?"

Ellis shoves him, pleased by how light the wiry creep feels. "Where is she?" he asks. "When she's not in Room 21, how do I get to her?"

"Please, sir," Arnie says. "I need to..."

"Tell me," Ellis hisses.

"I really can't. Ask Merl..."

"Did you fuck her?"

Arnie meets his gaze, flinching at the eye contact. "I told you, no."

"Then who has?"

A look passes over Arnie's long, equine face; a flicker of something terrible.

Ellis softens his voice, hoping to coax the truth from him. "It's very important that you tell me where she is."

"I can't."

"You don't need to be afraid of me..."

"I'm not afraid of *you*," Arnie says, and tries to barge past Ellis.

Ellis cracks his knuckles across Arnie's jaw. Pain shoots through Ellis' fingers and Arnie wails, high and childish.

"Shut the fuck up," Ellis says.

Arnie shields his face, whimpering. "I haven't done anything wrong."

Ellis raises his fist. "You really think that, don't you? All of you sick fuckers think that what you're doing here is good, fine, *normal*. Well it's not, and you need to recognize that. I've made my mistakes, but nothing like this!"

Arnie cowers. "I can't say anything. I'm not allowed! Why are you so mad?"

"Keep your voice down and just *tell me*."

"No! I'll get wet! I'll get wet!"

Ellis relaxes his arm and lets it fall, but inside he's churning, senses crackling and wild. "You'll get *wet*?"

Is Arnie afraid of ending up in a wetroom? There's only one guest that Ellis has seen who likes those places, whose leering face now fills his thoughts.

Yamamoto.

Emeley had stipulated 'no wetrooms' in her contract, but despite what Merl claimed when Ellis arrived, not much in this place seems to be above board. And though Yamamoto is the last person he wants to face, if Emeley is spending her final days with him, Ellis has no choice.

Arnie rubs his chin. "Can I go now?"

Ellis nods and reaches into his pocket for a generous tip. "You're safe from me if you keep your mouth shut." He holds out a hundred-dollar bill, the only one he has.

Arnie snatches the money. "Fine. Enjoy your gift, you...you asshole."

Ellis lets it go.

The tall, thin man passes him and leaves the room.

Ellis eyes the metal cloche on the desk. He wishes he could believe that it is a simple dessert or burger waiting under there, but that could hardly be considered a treat for a VIP guest at *this* motel. He wishes he could leave it a mystery.

He wonders, has Merl figured him out?

Emeley?

He lifts the lid and finds a woman's severed head—but not his wife's. The braided hair is blonde and the lips are too small, the eyes slightly closer together, the pores too big. The stump of its neck is sealed with some kind of gold cap resting on a bed of ice, and a folded card sits beneath its chin, bearing a note: *Rather than lose your head, how about you GET some head instead? Don't worry, she doesn't bite! - Merl.*

The decapitated dome's mouth is agape, propped open with a transparent silicone dental gag. Inside, a dark cavern. All the teeth have been pulled.

Ellis replaces the lid, trapping the spider under the cup.

This fucking place.

He'd burn it to the ground if he could.

Motel Styx

One of a kind

Visiting here should be on everyone's bucket list! Only motel I know where you can get a room both before and after you die.

In the Mouth of Utter Madness

Yamamoto opens his door nude, his expression as vibrant as a sun-ray.

Glee bursts from every feature: his intense eyes are wild, his pupils dilated, his cheeks dimpled, his mouth curved in delight and his perfect teeth as white as a heavy snowfall. Blood is smudged thick and treacly across his abdomen, and flecks of meat encrust his pubic hairs.

"Yes," the maniac says, as if he's been expecting Ellis.

Behind Yamamoto, the sliver of wetroom that Ellis can see is murky and dim. The smell of copper and bodily gasses issues from the gap.

"Welcome!" Yamamoto says, and widens the space between door and frame. "Please, come in."

Ellis pulls the gun and aims it at Yamamoto's face. He has a single moment to enjoy the power that pointing a weapon at a fellow human instills, then the world shifts on its axis.

The next thing Ellis knows is a hot pain stabbing his wrist, and then he's crumpled on the wetroom floor, the gun no longer in his hand. He realizes how ill-prepared he is when he sees that everything—*everything*—around him is horror.

Yamamoto towers above him and Ellis stares up into the barrel of the gun. The shock of having his life threatened with his own weapon slips out of focus when he hears something move to his left.

Near the wall, Damien sits naked and blood-drenched on a chair, gagged with black tape and with his arms strained behind him. He's alive, his eyes wider than should be possible, sitting stock-still. When Ellis sees that one of his brother-in-law's ears has been stripped from his skull along with part of his upper lip, he understands the nature of Damien's demented gaze: his eyelids have been snipped away. While the blood covering Yamamoto's body is smeared and erratic, Damien's blood seems as thick as a fresh coat of paint. His bare upper torso is strewn with lumps of skin affixed with lop-sided iron nails that have been pounded into his chest. Ellis recognizes the ear hammered to the right of one nipple, but the other scraps and streaks are impossible to identify. Damien's cell phone lies discarded at his feet.

Ellis scrabbles away from Yamamoto, palms skidding on the puddled floor. His spine bashes into the central embalming table where he'd seen the two women lying entangled the last time he was there. He leans back and a limp arm drapes itself over his shoulder. Screeching, he shoves it away. It flies off the table and hits the tiles, severed at the elbow.

Yamamoto clubs Ellis' mouth with the gun, breaking a front tooth and reminding him of the nightmarish fate the Christian protester had suffered at Yamamoto's hands earlier that day.

"I'm sssorry, I'm sssorry!" Ellis says, his S's now whistling, his head echoey with pain and terror.

"Stop, now," Yamamoto says. He points the gun at Damien. "Tell him."

Air rushes in and out of Damien's nose. His too-wide eyes look delirious as he nods frantically at Ellis, imploring him to cooperate.

"I'm sorry," Ellis says, holding one hand to his face and the other, palm-out, in surrender. "I don't care what you're doing..."

"Stop," Yamamoto says.

Ellis does.

Yamamoto points to a space beside Damien's chair. "There."

Ellis' thoughts reduce to a crawl. All his care, all his money, all his preparations were all for nothing. He scoots over, favoring his uninjured right hand over the throbbing left one which he hopes Yamamoto has not broken. Damien groans. Ellis looks up into his brother-in-law's duct-taped face: the crawling naked eyes, slashed forehead, battered cheeks, and grazed jaw. Ellis has no words of reassurance.

Yamamoto goes to the central table, and when Ellis sees the mangled shape lying there he has to stop himself from screaming again.

Still wearing her Café Charon uniform, *sans* nametag, the breakfast waitress Camila lies ruined and violated. Yamamoto has left her sweet face untouched: her round spectacles remain in place and her hair bun is as neat as it was that morning.

Camila lies on the table, her legs spread beyond their limits at 10 o'clock and 2 o'clock. They end at her ankles, where nubs of bone protrude from the ragged meat. Both lower arms have been removed, and while Ellis had thrown one of those severed limbs across the room, the other is buried wrist-deep in the bloodied folds between her open thighs. A glance at Camila's stomach reveals a gaping red crater where, for some unfathomable reason, her feet have been planted, toes poking from the hole like grubs emerging from a nest. A metal pail stands by the table, filled to the brim with a scarlet stew of extracted organs.

Beyond Ellis' dread he feels something worse: defeat. He'll never get to say his true goodbye to Emeley. He'll die here, and the last thing anyone will know about him is that he spent his last few days as a guest at a fucking necrotel.

"I was going to come to you," Yamamoto says, still training the gun on Ellis. Without looking, he reaches down with his other hand and caresses Camila's motionless face. "That's what I agreed: I do these two, then I come to you."

"What do you mean?" Ellis asks dully.

"I got mad this morning, in the café. That man had a big mouth, telling stories about me." Yamamoto lets his fingers drift down Camila's throat, between her clothed breasts, then lower still. "I shouldn't have been so angry. I have a trouble, you see. Temper trouble. Chris understands."

"Chris," Ellis murmurs.

"Yes, Chris. A good man. He helps me. He knows I think that dead is good, but that *alive and then dead* is better. The dead do not bleed like the living."

Ellis finally sees how the pieces fit together. "Chris supplies you with...people you can kill?"

The joyful leer re-emerges on Yamamoto's face. "Yes, *yes!* A very good man. He understands. Not like Merl. Merl is a businessman, but doesn't want trouble. Chris though—an opportunist! On some visits, I pay Chris more than I pay for my room!"

Ellis feels something rise up in his throat: laughter or a sob, he can't tell which. "Where...is she?" he pleads, his voice tremulous. "Where is she?"

"Who?" Yamamoto asks.

"My wife."

"A guest?"

"No."

Yamamoto blinks. "Your wife is one of the fuck-bodies?"

"You know she is," he says bitterly. "And I know you're staying in Room 21, because Arnie was afraid he'd 'get wet' if he told me."

"The morgue-man? I don't even know him."

"Liar!" he howls. *"Where's my fucking wife, Emeley?"*

Yamamoto shrugs. "I name them myself. This one here..." He glances at Camila. "This one is Aiko. And *this* is my room. I sleep over there." He points to a corner where a crumpled sleeping bag and a foam pillow lie amidst the bloody carnage.

The lunatic sleeps in this charnel house.

Ellis chokes on the lump in his throat. "Then where is she? Please tell me. Please."

Yamamoto clicks his tongue. "Chris said you've been looking around the motel, going places you shouldn't."

"Yes. Looking for my wife."

"He says you found something on the cameras."

"How did..." Ellis starts, but he already knows.

True to form, Veronika had told Chris everything. Ellis wouldn't be surprised if Chris knew all along who Ellis was. That woman is a manipulative fucking psycho.

There's not much to do out here in the middle of nowhere, she'd said. *Gotta take my fun wherever I can find it.*

"You're not a cop though, like Chris thinks," Yamamoto says. "You are a sad husband looking for his fuck-body wife! Very entertaining." The maniac looks at Camila's desecrated body. "All of us here at Motel Styx want something, don't we? Bodies of the living. Bodies of the dead." He grips the corpse's severed wrist and pushes the hand deeper into its birth canal. "Ever since I was a little boy, all I have wanted is a place to do exactly as I please."

Ellis can't look away, even when Yamamoto lowers the gun to reach into the gaping wound in Camila's belly. With a tearing sound, Yamamoto tugs, and the length of severed arm protruding between the corpse's thighs shortens. Like the hands of gore-glazed lovers, Yamamoto has interlinked his fingers with those at the end of Camila's severed arm. He pulls and her arm retracts into her straining vulva until all that remains there is a bony stump. Finally, it vanishes inside with a vacuumous pop.

Yamamoto removes the corpse's arm from the stomach and lifts it like a dripping, dangling prize. "I can do whatever I like here," he says, and drops Camila's limb to the filthy floor. "It's my playground. My...carnival. Do you know what it feels like, knowing you can do anything to someone?"

An image appears in his mind: Emeley, cowering and clutching her lower abdomen.

"I think that, maybe, you do," Yamamoto says. "Now go to your friend's chair and put your hands behind you."

Ellis turns to Damien and is about to do as he is asked when the familiar fury ignites in his chest, alongside the sensation that this chaotic world is moving *him*, instead of Ellis moving the world.

"You..." he growls, but not to Yamamoto: to Damien. "You *had* to come and screw things up, didn't you?"

If Damien hadn't pursued him to Motel Styx, then the protester wouldn't have overheard their conversation and approached them in Café Charon. That poor bastard's death set off a domino-sequence of events, which culminated in...this.

"Just go to the..." Yamamoto starts.

It's the anger that moves Ellis now, though, not the Earth. He's incensed and it melts away some of his fear, so he rages at Damien: "Why couldn't you have been more concerned for Emeley when she was *alive*? Why couldn't you have admitted to her that I was good for her? That I was helping her reach her true potential?"

"I..." Yamamoto says.

"Fuck you!" Ellis bellows.

Sensing his moment, he wheels around and launches himself at Yamamoto.

Yamamoto raises the gun but Ellis wraps his fingers around his aggressor's wrist and wrenches it towards him. The pistol slips from Yamamoto's bloody hand. Ellis stumbles on something but uses his clumsy momentum to fuel an attack: he clutches his other hand around Yamamoto's arm and yanks it down with full force, snapping the wrist against his thigh like one of Emeley's pencils he'd broken in the Greenlee Suite.

Yamamoto cries out and holds his arm to his bare chest. "Bastard!" he spits.

The gun lies on the floor between them, beside a half-smeared puddle of blood. Ellis dives, expecting a race, but instead Yamamoto backhands him with his un-injured fist. Ellis' head clashes with the table leg and a galaxy of stars soars across his vision. Lying on his back, dazed and half-submerged in something viscous, he watches Yamamoto reach down.

When Ellis sits up and snatches for the gun, they each get a hold of it: Ellis the barrel and Yamamoto the handle. They're so close to one another that Ellis consid-ers a headbutt, but he doesn't have the courage. Instead he drags Yamamoto towards him and bites the corded tendons between the man's throat and shoulder.

The man yells out and the gun once again skitters across the tacky floor. Yamamoto wrenches Ellis' hair back so that his chomping teeth withdraw and they tus-sle, intimately close, all nails and fists.

Despite his likely-broken wrist, Yamamoto is the dominant fighter. He clambers on top and digs a thumb into Ellis' windpipe, his hand padlock-tight around Ellis' throat.

With a surge of determination, Ellis jerks sideways. There's an appalling crash and Yamamoto's grip loosens, falling away as he collapses off Ellis. Ellis braces himself, the air whistling in and out of him, waiting for a count-er-attack that never comes.

Once he has regulated his breathing, he sits up.

Yamamoto's head has flopped into the bucket hold-ing Camila's internal organs. The man's limbs twitch and convulse but his face remains stuffed into the pail, face-first on a glistening red-and-pink bed. Ellis gets to his feet, unsteady, suspecting a trick. He stands over Yamamoto, watching the man's arms writhe and cheeks flop against Camila's innards. When Ellis rolled, he must have thrown Yamamoto's head into the side of the gurney, the blow more solid than Ellis could have hoped for.

A realization dawns on him: he has already passed barriers he never thought he would cross, and if he is ever going to feel safe again, he now has to cross another.

What goes on in Motel Styx, stays in Motel Styx.

He drives his knee into the back of Yamamoto's skull. His kneecap throbs at the impact but he keeps it pressed against his attacker's head even when the maniac's arms begin to flail. Submerged in coils and chunks of organic matter, Yamamoto thrashes like a fish pulled from a lake to die on the boards of a boat. Yamamoto struggles for minutes, drowning in his victim's viscera, but Ellis keeps the heavy pressure of his body against the man's cranium even after his movements have finally ceased.

When Ellis staggers to his feet, he realizes that his brother-in-law has been screaming behind his gag for a while now, the sound muffled but frantic.

"You need to stop panicking," Ellis says, feeling blood gumming up his fingers and tasting Yamamoto's chewed skin. "It won't help."

Behind the tape, Damien's insane panic drops to a grumble, as if the severity of his situation is dawning on him. The heavy nails in his chest need to be extracted. The hole where his ear once was will need countless stitches. And his eyelids? What the hell can be done about those?

Ellis circles Damien's chair and starts to unwrap his bound ankles. Fearing that his brother-in-law's cries will attract attention, he leaves the gag in place and wonders what else Yamamoto put him through—molestation? Rape?

"We're going to get you out of here, Damien," he says.

Damien's cries increase again, high and keening, and he slaps his black-taped hands against the wood of the chair.

"What is it?" Ellis asks.

His brother-in-law nods and points frantically at his lap.

All Ellis sees is Damien's penis and balls squashed above his bare thighs.

"What?" Ellis asks.

"Mmmmmmm-hunnnnn muuuuuh!"

Behind me.

With a sinking horror, Ellis goes to the rear of the seat.

The chair Damien is secured to is a piece of basic wooden dining furniture, with a gap between the padded backrest and seat. At first Ellis doesn't understand what he's seeing. Another nail has been hammered into the chair and stands propped between Damien's buttocks, but when Ellis crouches he sees a lump of something light pink. It looks like the head of a compressed frankfurter. When the smell hits his nose, sharp and pungent, he almost trips as he scrambles away.

Damien is doomed.

Damien is as good as dead.

Part of Damien's bowel has been tugged from his body and nailed to the chair.

"Oh," Ellis says.

Damien seems to hear the bleakness in Ellis' voice, and his body sags with the weight of it. His eyes lower to the floor and he squeezes a shuddering breath out through his nose. The man's arrogance and self-certainty has drained away, the exhaustion of bereavement and the trauma of his ordeal having stolen everything from him.

"You won't make it to a hospital," Ellis says, without emotion. "It's over 20 miles away, and I...I have something I still need to do."

Damien looks at him with imploring eyes. "Uh-is," he says, the black tape mangling Ellis' name. "Eesh."

Please.

"I can't," Ellis says.

He remembers how condescending and scornful his brother-in-law had always been towards him. Emeley confessed that Damien never liked him, and that Damien tried to dissuade her from marrying him, who Damien claimed had "no prospects".

A streak of malice runs through Ellis. "Who's out of prospects now?"

Damien looks up, face creased with despair.

"I can't do anything for you," Ellis says. "You never should have come."

He goes to the door, leaving Camila and her jumble of dead limbs, the suffocated corpse of Yamamoto, and the bleeding remnants of his brother-in-law.

"*Eeesh!*" Damien begs, waving one weak, bound hand. "*Eeeeeeeeeeeesh!*"

Ellis picks up the gun, takes one final look at the man nailed to the chair, and leaves the wetroom.

Motel Styx

"

They took my son. I know they did. Won't anyone help?
If you know what's really happening at Motel Styx please
please please DM me.

"

- DesperateMom1982, r/necro, Reddit

Room 21

The silenced gun kicks against Ellis' palm with a stiff *BOM*.

With one well-aimed shot the door swings wide, and Ellis is finally admitted to Room 21.

Chris sits on a king-size double bed in a plain, simple motel room, and his head jerks up when Ellis shoves his way inside.

"You," Ellis says. "*You.*"

"Hi, Mac," Chris says, seemingly unperturbed. "Why didn't you just knock?"

Chris is alone in the room; no Emeley.

"Fuck you, Chris," Ellis says, his mind fraught and haywire. "Where is she?"

"Emeley?" Chris asks, his voice faux-innocent.

"Your little wifey?"

Ellis pushes the door shut behind him and holds Chris in the gun's sights. "Veronika has been feeding you everything about me, hasn't she?"

Chris shrugs. "I don't know about *everything*—you never can tell with her, coz she loves playing games. But she told me enough to keep herself amused."

"Does Merl know?"

Chris shrugs again. "Not from me."

"Tell me where she is."

Chris angles his head, looking genuinely curious. "Why do you care so much, Mac? She's just a body. She took her own life too, didn't she, just to get away from you? Seems disrespectful to deny her last request."

Ellis has had enough: he crosses the room with a few quick strides and slams the gun into Chris' skull.

The Head of Security's expression shifts into shock and he topples sideways onto the bed, his temple releasing a trickle of blood. With his cheek pressed into the pillow, he groans and cups the fresh wound with his palm.

Ellis points the gun at Chris' chest. "I care because what happens in here isn't fucking *right*. Everyone has lost their minds."

"Emeley asked for it," Chris says, pulling himself upright. "She literally signed a contract: now why would she do that if it was goin' to upset her beloved so much, huh?"

"*I'm done talking!*" Ellis yells, and rams the handle of the gun into Chris' jaw.

Chris makes no attempt to block the blow: the lower part of his face jams crooked, knocking his bloody grin strange and obscene.

He likes it, Ellis' mind gibbers. *It turns him on...*

"But seriously, Mac," Chris says, in a voice distorted by his lop-sided head. He sits straight up, bleeding from his brow and busted mouth. "Why'd your wife let me fuck all her holes?"

Ellis' vision dampens. "I'll shoot you, Chris. I'll kill you if you push me."

Chris takes his jaw in both hands and slots it back with a gristly click. "You know, I think you really might."

"Then where?" Ellis says.

"Haven't you got anything else to ask me about this place? You've been doing so much digging and this might be your last chance."

Ellis hesitates. He's right. There's no going back now, so for one moment he gives in to his curiosity about the secrets of Motel Styx. If he makes it out alive, maybe he can use it all against them. "How are you supplying people to Yamamoto? Why doesn't anyone come looking?"

Chris wipes his lip. "Not everyone tells their friends and family they're coming to a goddamn necrotel. All payments are taken through secured links. We pick the lone ones, or the especially pesky protesters, then their cars are stripped and junked over 200 miles away, their other belongings incinerated." The sick fuck's eyes glint with pride. "Merl thinks the guests we pick check out early, but, *poof.* They just disappear."

"You piece of *shit.*"

Chris spits blood. "I've worked for bad people, I've seen some things, and sure, I've helped Yamamoto out. But I've *never* hurt a woman, Mac. Not like you."

Ellis fumbles for words. "Is...is that why Emeley wasn't in Merl's binder?"

"Of course! You beat her tits and stomach so bad before she died she looked like an old banana. Can't offer up a body like that to the clientele! She was only fit for the wetrooms, but she said 'no dismemberment' in her contract and according to Merl, consent is important! Lucky me though: I get first choice of the throwaways, perk of the job, so I owe you and your temper a thank-you."

No.

It *can't* be his fault that Emeley ended up in Chris' bed.

Emeley drove him to every one of those bruises.

"Real interesting type of love you had there. Did she like it that rough?"

"Where is she?"

With one half of his face slathered in blood, Chris offers a cruel smile. "Almost free of you. Right now, Arnie is burning her in the crematory. I doubt there's anything left."

"She's not due to be cremated yet! I saw the date."

"She's past her prime, all used up, so I moved it to today. Another perk of the job: total fucking control."

"*Motherfucker!*" Ellis yells.

He swings the gun again, smashing it against Chris' cheek with a sharp crack. His eyes roll and he slumps onto the bed, still at last.

Ellis searches his pockets, finds his keycard, and flees the room, desperate to find Emeley before the flames claim her for good.

Back in the corridor, something wails. In Ellis' dizzy haste he thinks that the sound is a ringtone or an alarm, but when he turns towards the office and crematory, he sees a bloodied figure limping away from him, leaking a constant stream of dark liquid as it hobbles down the corridor. Ellis sees a pink tube dangling free from between its asscheeks to its upper thighs.

Damien, a gruesome wreck, turns back to Ellis. Tape no longer secures his legs or gags his mouth, and in a ragged voice, Ellis' brother-in-law gasps, "*You son of a bitch.*"

Knowing that time is against him, Ellis sprints as though a starting pistol had been fired. Damien raises his arms but Ellis is a battering ram, a speeding bulldozer. He plows into his brother-in-law without mercy, charging with his right shoulder forwards so that it crashes into Damien's weak, outstretched arms. Something snaps and Damien is sent flying, like a scarecrow in a hurricane.

Ellis barrels on towards the vestibule, tearing through the door marked *Staff Only* and following the corridor towards the refrigerator.

Now he slows, panting. A smell stops him in his tracks, a scent so rich with *déjà vu* that teardrops well in his eyes. He couldn't describe the sweet aroma if he tried, but he would recognize its faintest wisp anywhere.

Emeley.

Someone will soon be in pursuit, but for now he hears nothing behind him. He holds Chris' keycard up to the lock and eases open the entrance to the warehouse proper. The door to the crematory is ajar, allowing a low, chugging sound of machinery and the stink of char and fumes to escape.

"Oh fuck."

Ellis bursts through the door.

"Stop! Don't you dare burn her!"

Arnie is *not* burning her.

As is his way, Arnie has Ellis' dead wife lying on her front on a gurney. Although he still wears a white shirt, he has dragged his pants down to his ankles. His considerable rod is stiff in one hand, and with the other he is spreading Emeley's buttocks apart, pulling open her holes as though preparing to stuff a turkey.

Ellis' wife is an object to Arnie; a series of cold entrances.

Forget 'til death do us part'.

"I tried not to, but..." Arnie begins.

"You should have taken my advice."

Ellis lifts the gun and fires.

Arnie stumbles backwards, feet snagging in his pulled-down pants. He looks confused as he clutches the bloodied hole in his chest, blinking, opening his lips without making a sound. Then the muscles in his face fall slack. With a colossal crash he falls into a cabinet topped with books and metal tools, and slides blankly to the floor.

Ellis looks at Emeley, his wife, expecting a surge of emotion, but feels only the urgency to leave well up in him.

"I found you," he says, pacing towards her. "I made it all the way here and I fucking found you."

Love is fleeting

*If one night stands with frigid women is your thing, you'll
love it here. Just don't fall in love because all of these
women will leave you, guaranteed.*

Reunion

Hoisted over his shoulder, Ellis' wife is ponderous and
heavy as he waits for the upwards-rolling door of the
warehouse space to open. When it clears his head, he
hurries into the dusty twilight behind the motel and follows the perimeter of the building to the private car park.

"You're a *dead weight*, Emeley," he says under his
breath, feeling giddy, and when something inside her
sloshes in reply a wild giggle slips from him.

It's quiet, with no members he can see to spot him
carrying his strange cargo.

He'd swaddled Emeley in a stained sheet he'd found
in the corner of the crematory room. Even with her head
draped halfway down his back, her stench fills his nose:
spice and rot; sulfur and semen; postmortem chemicals
and a waft of cherry blossom. But beneath the horror
of those conflictions he can smell the essential *her*, that
indescribable tang that always kept him loyal, obsessed

227

even; mentally, though not always physically.

Clutching Chris' keycard, he hurries to the electronic lock that seals the parking lot he'd entered only yesterday. It bleeps and he scans the vehicles for his car. At first he can't remember where he'd left the rental but then there it is, unlit and tint-windowed, waiting for his escape. Except there's something wrong: it's leaning at an odd angle.

As the motion-detected lights flicker on, Ellis sees that the tires are deflated and gouges of rubber have been pulled back like incised skin.

"The *fuck*?"

Keeping Emeley steady, he digs into his holster and retrieves the gun.

"Chris?" he calls, teetering under her weight. "Merl?"

He glances at the car again and considers trying to drive regardless, but in his mind he hears the grating squeal of the tires against gravel and desert dirt, and remembers an old video of a woman driving with a flat that had burst into flames. He imagines Merl and his lackeys circling him in the struggling vehicle, shattering a window, and dragging him through the jagged gap.

"Shit, shit, shit," he says, scanning the parking lot again. "I've got a gun, you fuckers! If you follow me, I'll shoot—don't think I won't!"

Despite a new spike of adrenaline he can hear the weariness in his voice, the wavering notes of hysteria. He's risked everything, fraternized with perverts, and even murdered two men, and for what?

A rotting corpse.

A wife turned whore.

"I can't believe the things I've done for you, Emeley," he mutters. "Are you happy now?"

He opens the rental's trunk and retrieves the shovel he'd bought after securing the gun the day before, then rushes away with his wife's body sagging against him. Glancing left and right for signs of the tire-slasher he hurries around the perimeter of Motel Styx, feeling Emeley's head flop against his spine.

Whatever happens, he won't be coming back, even if he has to die frozen and alone in the desert. The temperature feels almost comfortable by Texas standards this early evening, but when the sun disappears completely he'll be shivering and exposed. If he can make it off the property uncontested, the darkening dusk will work in his favor.

Where can he go, though? The protesters' encampment? Chris and Yamamoto have been picking the most vocal Christians off and dragging them to the wetrooms, somehow evading Merl's gaze, so surely *they'd* protect him.

But while he's not exactly a happy customer of Motel Styx, he's no longer a prude to the uses of the dead, is he? Despite retaining his corpse-virginity, he now straddles the gulf between necs and normies. And if the protesters demand that he abandons Emeley in exchange for their protection, will he?

Of course not.

So he hauls ass away from both the motel and the Christian base camp, towards a greener area of desert. Succulents and cacti clamber from the flat arid surface, and yuccas like green clumps of swords impale the evening air. The sky is a dim electric blue but there's still plenty of light with which to see the tents, trucks, and SUVs. The activists themselves are sitting around a fire to eat. He can hear a woman strumming a guitar and singing an old, haunting hymn with a scratchy voice. The sound fills him with melancholy. Emeley used to sing like that when she was in the shower: tuneless but full of verve.

"Couldn't sing for shit, could you, Em?" he says, as he treads further into the sandy wasteland. "Must admit I liked hearing it, though."

There's still no sign that he's being pursued. Maybe Merl has enough on his hands already after the chaos Ellis had caused, and bigger priorities than saving what he would surely see as a used-up corpse: his morgue assistant bleeding out on the floor of the crematory, his Head of Security nursing a concussion, a mutilated man wandering the halls. If Ellis can find cover behind the plants and desert rises, he'll be able to walk parallel with the main road and find it again by morning. He'll head for Valentine, that's what he'll do. The town will love another reason to hate the motel.

If that's true, then who slashed your tires?

Pushing the thought aside, he walks until he is exhausted and the sky has dipped to a silvery gray, peppered with stars. He needs to rest but first he has to say a proper goodbye, so he jams the shovel upright into the dirt and lays his wife down on the stony ground. Nodding solemnly, he lowers himself to a crouch beside her.

In the dying light, the sheet smothers Emeley's face and skin like a mummy. He peels the material, tacky with spilled secretions, away from her forehead, nose, and mouth to get a good look at her. Her new eyes look wrong; Merl couldn't match their color with painted glass.

With the sheet still covering her nudity, Emeley gazes back at her husband.

Ellis sits down cross-legged beside her, reaches beneath the material, and takes one of her hands. She's cold and there's no comfort in her touch. He almost lets go, but instead pulls his wallet from his pocket and takes out Emeley's wedding ring, which she'd left on the edge of the tub in their apartment for him to find next to her corpse. Tugging her hand out from beneath the sheet, he places the gold band back onto her death-stiffened finger, where it belongs.

"You're still mine," he says, but his voice is tired and marred by grief. He traces his finger across the small scar above one of Emeley's eyebrows. A scar he gave her. A reminder of their tensions.

The wind rises with a shrill whistle.

He's unsure what to say, now he's alone with her. She's no longer attractive in any conventional way and there's a sickly darkness around her eye sockets. The texture of her blued skin reminds him of a store mannequin, but it's still her; she's still Emeley.

My Emeley.

"I keep thinking about that last conversation," he manages. "I keep wondering if I should've known, you know? You just looked sleepy to me, and you'd been that way since...well, since you lost her. So when I kissed you on the head before I went to work, and you looked all teary-eyed and said, 'Bye, Ellis,' I just thought, here we go again. Another day in paradise."

He squeezes her responseless hand and her joints crackle like pig fat.

"You never knew how to make the most of yourself. You always held back. That's why your business failed, and that's why you pissed away all your savings. That wasn't my fault. If you'd just pushed a little harder, you could have made it."

He stares at her lips, which have peeled back into a sneer so alien to his living wife's placid face. She always, wisely, kept her disapproving looks to herself, but in death her expression has turned accusatory.

In a moment of weakness, Ellis says, "Don't look at me like that, Em. I did my best, so why wasn't that enough? Every married couple goes through rough patches."

The sneer remains.

Ellis huffs. "Mom was right about you. You don't even know how lucky you were to have me. A lot of men would have been far tougher on you, so why, Em? Why would you do *this?*"

As she had in life, Emeley says nothing in reply—but he hears her loud and clear.

You know exactly why, her silence says. *Stop kidding yourself, you vicious prick.*

"You had so much fucking potential, but you squandered it. You could have been special, so you can't blame me for reacting sternly once in a while." He touches her forehead, her cheeks, her delicate mouth. "Can you imagine how bad you'd have gotten, if I let you? All that sitting around, all that shit sugary food? What a waste. You *needed* to be pushed."

Whenever he'd pushed her too hard, she covered up for him. Concealer hid most of the marks he left, but if they were too severe then she conjured a convincing story. Despite both of them knowing the facts, she would first tell Ellis her new version of the event—"The cupboard swung back too fast" or "I walked into a corner"—and if Ellis agreed, she would have permission to tell the same lie to other people. If her tales were believed, their apartment was an architecture in violence, with every entry and bend out for Emeley's blood.

Now, with her twisted mouth and rubbery skin, she seems less willing to keep their private life between them. The medical examiner washed off all the concealer, and she looks resentful, *vengeful*. That's what this whole nonsense has been about: hitting back at him. She'd chosen to die to prove a point.

Well, Ellis had given her a counter-argument, hadn't he? He'd traveled all this way, resisted being corrupted by the motel's body-fucking perverts, and found her again.

He pulls the sheet all the way off her naked flesh, which is discolored by both rot and the bruises he'd inflicted the night before she'd taken her own life. The marks are worse than he'd imagined; a cruel gathering of black and blue, like thick smoke or ink-stains across fabric.

Ellis takes the creased envelope from his back pocket and opens it. She'd taken the fatal overdose ten days prior and he'd found her note two days later, tucked away in a gym bag which Emeley knew he wouldn't use until at least Wednesday, his next regular workout day. He now knows that she'd timed it so her body would already be on its way to Motel Styx from the morgue, impossible for him to intercept.

He reads:

Ellis,

You were always saying you wanted me to toughen up, to grow a pair, to stop wasting my life. I tried so hard to be who you wanted. I changed and gave up so much. I loved you, Ellis. I still love you, but last month broke

me and there's no coming back from it. I'm done try-
ing.

Don't come looking for me.

You won't like what you find. I've made sure of that.

I was happy before I knew you. I had a job I loved, I
had savings, and I was content just being me.

So fuck you, Ellis. Fuck your control and your anger,
and fuck your mommy issues. Fuck your ego and your
goddamn superiority complex. Fuck you for making
me doubt myself. And fuck you for killing our sweet,
sweet girl, before she even saw daylight.

You can't hurt me anymore. I've taken that power
away.

But I sure can hurt you.

She hadn't even signed it.

Ellis rips the last remaining connection he has to his
living wife in two, then four, and then into a storm of
scraps he lets float on the desert breeze; scattered ashes
of their troubled partnership.

"You made your point, and now I've made mine," he
says. "You don't get to decide how this ends. *I do.*"

He drags himself to his feet and reaches for the shovel. Glancing around the clear, dark night, he wonders if
he'd heard a scuffling sound, then tells himself it's just
desert vermin, a snake or a bird. He won't be interrupted.

As Ellis digs, his wife's curled lips maintain their accusation.

"Don't look at me like that, Em," he says, ramming the shovel into the dirt. "Do you think that someone like *you* would have made a good mother? You could barely take care of yourself."

Emeley's silence is reply enough.

"We didn't have the money to feed a baby, after your shitty business choices!"

He recommences his work but catches sight of her face again.

"You're not the only one who lost her. How could I have known?" he asks. "I only pushed you, Em. It's not like I socked you in the gut. I fucking *pushed you*, that's all, but you went sprawling like a toddler. Now I know you're smaller than me, but Jesus Christ, it was like you'd *meant* to do it. So you went belly-first into the kitchen island—and you knew I never liked where you insisted on putting that thing, didn't you? You were pregnant, for fuck's sake, so why weren't you more careful?"

Digging her grave is hard, but unloading his pent-up wrath at last feels good.

"So, you bled, you cried, you went to the doc, and you squeezed out our dead daughter. Congratulations! Thanks for nothing! Lost potential, all over again. I could have made you into something special, the perfect wife."

It's darker now, but the half-moon and the distant, dying stars light Emeley's face, illuminating her disgust.

He turns with a snarl. "You know what? Fuck you too, Em. You don't get to judge me anymore. You don't get to blame me. You don't get to take the power away—*I'll always have it!*"

He brings the blade of the shovel down into the center of Emeley's face. It sinks all the way to the back of her skull, dividing her nose, cheek, and half of one eye socket.

"I bit my tongue throughout our marriage, but you know what? You were always a simpering cunt who couldn't thrive, even with my guidance. Born into a family of losers, and raised to be just like them." He retrieves the tool with a sucking thud, then brings it down into her chest. The shovel half-penetrates her breastplate. He wiggles it free with a thin dribble of embalming fluid then slams it into her stomach, her thighs, her arms, and her cold, useless genitals.

"Slut! Giving yourself to those motel freaks! Was that what you always wanted? To fuck perverts like Chris, to let them use you? Did you like his dick in you? Was it better than mine?"

He returns the shovel to her face, smashing the tool again and again until the flesh peels away and parts of her skull gleam in the desert moonlight.

"You disgust me, you fucking whore!"

After his scream fades, he stops, the shovel standing at a loose angle, its metal edge buried in his wife's shattered forehead.

Then, just like the times his anger got the better of him during their marriage, and he'd slapped her, or punched her, or throttled her, Ellis fills with tumultuous regret.

She used to call him a flip-flopper.

His mom said he was better than that.

He drops to his knees.

"I'm sorry, Em. I don't mean it. You *were* better than that, I know you were."

He lays his hands on her ruined chest, feeling for

the heartbeat he knows isn't there.

"I'm sorry. You know how I get. You press my buttons like no one else can, but that just shows how much I love you, doesn't it? You understand that, right? You always did."

Emeley lies in fragments, her face chopped into mismatched jigsaw pieces, her chest and stomach open, her pussy split into bulbous ribbons. He feels so much remorse, even more than when she'd lost their baby, so he leans over and kisses her demolished mouth, feeling her broken teeth and torn skin against his lips.

No matter how different she is now, she's still his Emeley.

He clambers between her ripped, bloodless thighs, preparing to heal them both, just as he always did whenever she pushed him so hard that he lashed out. She never fought back afterwards, even if he made her bleed, and he would relish her terror as he made his apologetic love to her, knowing that her fear meant she was his and his alone.

So that's just what he does again now.

His wife's body has never felt so welcoming. He knows this is the last time he'll ever have her—the last time *anyone will*—so he takes his time, kissing her segmented features, sliding his fingers across her taut breasts and, even more intimately, inside the slashed spaces he'd carved open with the shovel. They've never been as close as they are when he reaches into the places he couldn't access when she was still alive. He smells the cold storage and decomposition of her chemically embalmed insides, but he also smells the *Emeley*, the *wife*, the *possession*.

Dimly, like a storm-shrouded horizon, he knows what he's doing is unnatural, but it's with tenderness that he fucks her—tenderness, and hate, and a desire to bury his dick alongside his guilt before he buries her rotting remains.

This is nothing like the actions of the necs back at the motel.

This is special.

This is love.

"You're so beautiful after I hurt you," he gasps.

He thinks of her crying and cowering from his hands, holding her ears from his berating, and it is with these images that Ellis cums, with his fist stuffed inside his wife's abdomen, seeking the hollow that once housed their miscarried baby. With a final, vicious kiss he chomps through and spits out her tongue, pumping his sperm into her vacant, bloodless hole.

"I love you," he says.

But in a sudden post-orgasm clarity, he hears the hollowness of the words as they fade into the otherwise empty desert.

Then the world vanishes in a flash of agony.

Perfect

I wish I could stay forever.

The Third Body

It's misty, wherever he is now. He must be dreaming because he can't quite feel his legs or arms. No, wait, he can *feel* them, but he can't *move* them.

The room slowly comes into focus, and at first he thinks he's having an out-of-body-experience in his dream, because he's staring into his own lidded eyes. It isn't astral projection, though—it's a mirror, much like the one from the desk in the Greenlee Suite, or even the mirror from that cramped airplane bathroom before he'd touched down in Texas.

Ellis is lying on his front, naked, with one cheek pressed to a sheet of cold steel and his blurry eyes unmoving as they gaze at the reflecting surface. He tries to rouse himself but can't shift his limbs. He can barely even move his eyes.

Is he even breathing?

"He came round to my way of doing things, Mac," a voice says.

With a plunging sensation, Ellis recognizes two

things: Chris' voice, and the surroundings of the wetroom.

"Merl, I mean," Chris says, and appears in the mirror, topless, behind Ellis' motionless head. His face is red, black, and scabbed from the assault Ellis committed on him back in Room 21, where he'd thought he'd find his wife, where she'd spent so much time. "Merl's a businessman at heart, as you know. Not a bad guy like Yamamoto, but smart and keen to make Motel Styx work, whatever that entails. So we'll blame Yamamoto for everything that happened tonight, and clear up the rest of the evidence...and witnesses."

When Chris runs his rough fingers across Ellis' bare shoulders, Ellis feels his touch but can't speak, can't move, and can't stop what's happening. It's not a dream.

"Probably seems like days have gone by since I knocked you out back in the desert, but it's only been a few hours. I dragged you to the motel myself, then came back and picked up the pieces of your lovely wife too."

Chris goes to the mirror, grins, and turns the angle of the glass.

Ellis wants to cry out at the waking nightmare reflected there.

Damien, mutilated and dead, is propped on a chair with a pile of human body parts draped over his thighs. In pieces, from her brother's lap, Emeley stares at Ellis with her one remaining eye.

"Thought you might get a little comfort if they were in here, keeping you company. A fucking family reunion! Should we be expecting more? Does anyone else know you're here, down among the necrophiles? You don't strike me as someone who would have many true friends."

Veronika laughs behind him.

Ellis fights to activate his muscles again but all he can do is stare, shifting his eyes fraction by fraction about the room. Even those delicate muscles seem to be seizing up.

"I'm guessing there's no cavalry," Chris says. "Now, you may be wondering if you're dead, or something, but you aren't. You've just had a shot of Merl's nec drug."

"SynthaMort! Love that name," Veronika says. She looks at Chris. "I want to have him both ways. Can I?"

"Whatever you want, baby." Chris waves a hand over Ellis' face. "He's here now, but he sure as shit won't be by the end."

Veronika steps into view behind Ellis' reflection. She's naked and holding a long-toothed handsaw. She looks at Chris. "We won't need lube to get in there, because once I start on him with this he'll bleed like a geyser."

She lowers the tool and Ellis feels the metal jaws scrape the small of his back, then down to the top of his ass crack.

Veronika looks up and makes eye contact with Ellis in the mirror. "Do you see that? *Look at yourself!*" she says, mocking the words he'd directed at her earlier that same day. "I've known other men like you, ones that liked to try and push me about, hit me. I'm going to enjoy this."

A tear falls from one of Ellis' eyes.

"And you'll be leaving here with Emeley, just like you wanted: straight out the chimney. I read her suicide note while you were showering, and she told you not to come here. I bet you wish you'd listened to her, for once."

Chris clears his throat. "I'm not usually into guys, but I'm gonna make an exception for you, Mac. I saw the damage you did to your wifey, so it's only right we give her a good show." Chris holds up the severed head Merl sent to Ellis' room and pulls the plastic, donut-holed gag from its mouth. He pries open Ellis' jaws and forces it between his teeth. "That's better."

You're better than this, Ellis hears his mom say, as Chris unbuttons his jeans.

You're better than this, he remembers telling Emeley, as he stares at her remains, her shattered face almost seeming to smirk.

You're better than this, he tells himself, as Veronika drags the tool's metal teeth down between his buttocks.

"I should give you *some* credit, Ellis: you're a changed man!" Veronika adds, as she begins to saw. "You fucked a corpse! You're one of us!"

Thank you for staying at Motel Styx!
Tell us about your stay

About Michelle von Eschen

Michelle von Eschen (early works written as Michelle Kilmer) is an American author of quiet, literary horror and dark, speculative fiction. Her works include Old Farmhouses of the North (a short story collection), Motel Styx (a collaborative novel), and much more.

She is a lover of the macabre who prefers Earl Grey tea, October, people who say goodbye on the phone, and her dreams are so real she can't figure out what has really happened to her. When she isn't writing, Michelle enjoys weightlifting, dark beer, web design, singing and playing guitar, and watching horror movies. She lives in England with her husband, horror author Jonathan Butcher.

About Jonathan Butcher

Jonathan Butcher is an English author of boundary-pushing fiction. His work tends to be extreme, at least in part, but later this year he'll be releasing something rather different.

Jonathan lives in south-west England with his wife and fellow horror author Michelle (pen names: Michelle von Eschen and Michelle Kilmer). But you know that already because she wrote this book with me – duh.

Also by
Michelle von Eschen

Novels
When the Dead

Novellas
The Spread
Mistakes I Made During the Zombie Apocalypse

Short Story Collections
Last Night While You Were Sleeping
When You Find Out What You're Made Of
Once Upon a Time, When Things Turned Out Okay
Old Farmhouses of the North

Individual Short Stories
When You Become a Body
This is How We Burn

Nonfiction
The Murk of Us

Edited Anthologies
GIVE: An Anthology of Anatomical Entries

With Other Publishers
The Cavity Wall | Dead Girls and Dead Things from
Books of Horror Presents
Wildflower | Screams of Sisterhood from Shadow House
Press

I'll Come Back | Roms, Bombs, and Zoms from Evil
Girlfriend Media
The World Wasn't Won | A Very Zombie Christmas from
ATZ Publications
Mora | Don't Cry to Mama from Jolly Horror Press
The Hands Resist Him | Accursed from Jolly Horror
Press

―――――――――――

Also by
Jonathan Butcher

Your Loved Ones Will Die First

What Good Girls Do (Elizabeth #1)

What Good Men Do (Elizabeth #2)

CHOCOLATEMAN

The Children at the Bottom of
the Gardden

Something Very Wrong
(collection)

Filthy Secrets (novelette)

...and much more coming soon

Acknowledgments

From Michelle:
This novel has been in the making for two years, since the day Jonathan and I watched *Nekromantik* together online while married, but still living some 5,000 miles apart. The movie was the first I'd seen to make me gag and from there, a new fascination was born. Thank you, Jörg Buttgereit, for twisting my stomach and mind and thank you Reddit, where someone mentioned consent before death as a way to decriminalize necrophilia. I haven't really been able to stop thinking about the motel since.

Thank you to my husband, who eagerly dove into the world I'd created and with this collaboration helped me truly bring it to life.

To the few friends and family we let onto the concept in its early days, I appreciate your willingness to listen, your endless support of our bizarre undertakings, and your ability to keep a secret!

To the incredible authors—Duncan Ralston, Judith Sonnet, Danger Slater, Bridgett Nelson, MJ Mars, and Megan Stockton—who agreed to read this book right after we finished it, we are indebted.

I'd also like to send my appreciation to two fellow authors who have been extremely supportive of my writing over the years, Jonathan Lambert and Tessa Stransky (@booksasmeals on IG). The feedback I've received from both of you has propelled me forward.

And to every reader who stays awhile at our motel and leaves a review about the experience, you're the absolute fucking best.

From Jonathan:

Naeem, for the gift that keeps on giving; Mum, and Dad in my heart; my author friends who continue to offer support and a willingness to read my filth, especially Matt Shaw, Duncan Ralston, Ryan Harding, Kristopher Triana, Megan Stockton, Stuart Bray, MJ Mars, and Kelvin Allison; readers and reviewers who recommend my work to others such as Alysha Yuhas, Eve Bullett, Christina Pfeiffer, Candace Nola, Corrina Morse, Crystal Cook, Jessica Shelly, and no doubt loads I've forgotten (sorry); Razr Candy for drawing crazy goddamn pictures of Kreb; and friends Chris Rollason, Dan Billing and Joe Allard for offering feedback when I need it. Thanks to Bree Tanner and several other helpful Redditors for invaluable insights into the work of morticians.

Oh, and you, Michelle, for letting me play in and expand your horrid concept.

Made in United States
Troutdale, OR
10/27/2024

24150313R00152